PECOS TRAIL

PECOS TRAIL

by

Mace Edwards

Dales Large Print Books
Long Preston, North Yorkshire,
BD23 4ND, England.

British Library Cataloguing in Publication Data.

Edwards, Mace
  Pecos trail.

    A catalogue record of this book is
    available from the British Library

    ISBN   978-1-84262-816-4 pbk

First published in Great Britain 1983 by Robert Hale Limited

Copyright © Jim Bowden 1983

Cover illustration © Michael Thomas

The moral right of the author has been asserted

Published in Large Print 2011 by arrangement with
Mr W. D. Spence

Dales Large Print is an imprint of Library Magna Books Ltd.

Printed and bound in Great Britain by
T.J. (International) Ltd., Cornwall, PL28 8RW

ONE

In spite of the hot Texas sun Jim Hooper shivered.

Things were not as they should be. He sensed it in his bones.

Checking his horse, he sat motionless. His dark brown eyes beat through the distance, trying to penetrate the heat-haze and stop the house dancing in an out-of-focus picture.

Jim cursed the heat. He wanted a clearer scene. He had viewed the familiar as he had crossed the ridge on to the quarter-mile wide incline which sloped gently to the house half-a-mile away beside the quietly flowing waters of the Rio Grande. In that first sweeping glance everything looked the same as when he had left three days ago to search for mustangs. But then, as he moved on to the sloping ground and the shimmering disturbed the picture, an uneasy feeling had swept into him.

He tapped his horse forward and moved slowly down the slope until he reached a point where the irritating dance ceased and the house stood out sharp and clear.

The lines on Jim's weatherbeaten face were multiplied by the worry which gnawed at him as he stopped his mount once again. His square jaw tightened and muscles twitched in anxiety. There was a stillness around the house which seemed charged with foreboding.

Kate! Her name screamed into his mind.

Normally she would have been coming to greet him, for any movement on this slope could easily be seen. That was why Jim had built the house where he had. With the ridge swinging round in both directions to end in steep bluffs along the river, the slope offered the only approach to the house.

He had chosen the site carefully three years ago when he and Kate had come to the

south-west of Texas after she had successfully persuaded him to give up his job as
sheriff of Rosewell County. At forty she had
seen his reactions showing the first signs of
slowing. She realised that one day one of the
criminals who had sworn revenge on his
captor, or one of the gun-crazy youngsters
out to prove he was faster than the great Jim
Hooper, would outdraw her husband. It had
been a hard task to persuade him but she
had eventually succeeded. Jim had had to
admit that he was attracted by the prospect
of a quiet life together, tucked away where
nobody would find them, and the chance to
round up mustangs.

Life had been good. Nothing had disturbed
it until now.

Kate!

Jim stabbed his horse into a fast gallop
down the remainder of the slope towards the
house. The hoofbeats pounded her name in
his mind as he tried to convince himself that
she was all right.

He was out of the saddle almost before his

mount slid to a dust-stirring halt in front of the one-storey building. He took the four steps on to the verandah in two strides and flung the door open with a crash. His wife's name froze unuttered on his lips as the scene struck him.

Three well-built Mexicans were sitting at the table forking food quickly into their mouths while Kate, her face pale with an unmistakable anxiety, served them.

As soon as Jim strode into the room, Kate flung herself at him, burying her head against his chest and sobbed with relief in the protection of his strong arms.

'What the hell's going on, Diaz?' Jim's eyes flashed with an angered fury at the Mexican who leaned back on his chair grinning broadly at him.

Diaz did not answer but reached forward, without taking his eyes off Jim, and closed his broad hairy hand around a mug which stood beside his plate almost cleared of food. He raised it to his lips letting the wine slop down the sides of his mouth as he gulped it down. He chuckled deep in his throat as he slammed the mug down on the table.

'Nice greeting from ze wife,' he grinned. 'She want to come when we heard your horse but I couldn't let her. You understand, Senor Jim?'

'Cut it out Diaz,' broke in Jim. 'Answer my question.'

'Aw, you are angry. You call me Diaz when you are angry.' He spread his hands in mock protest. 'Please, Fernandez like you do when we are friendly.'

'Hell, of course I'm angry. You take over my house with two of your filthy sidekicks, my wife is frightened. What the hell do you expect me to be?'

'Come, sit down and we'll talk.' Diaz extended his hand towards a chair on the opposite side of the table.

Jim glanced down at Kate who had straightened and was wiping the tears from her eyes though she still clung close to her husband. 'What's it all about, Kate?'

'He arrived yesterday wanting you. I told

him you'd be back today and he insisted on waiting.'

'He was here all night?' gasped Jim.

'It was all right, Senor Jim,' put in Diaz quickly. 'I would not let my two friends do anything,' he added with a grin and a wink. 'I insisted on waiting because I want to be here when you arrive. It's important.'

Two strides took Jim to the table and the nearest Mexican. Before the man realised what was happening Jim grasped him firmly by the collar and, yanking him out of the chair, he spun round and hurled him towards the door. 'Get this scum out of here and I'll talk with you,' yelled Jim as he turned sharply towards the other Mexican. The man's hand had started to move towards the pistol on the table but Diaz was quicker and his huge hand closed over the weapon first.

His dark eyes flashed at his sidekick. 'No! I need Senor Hooper. Go.'

The man scrambled hurriedly to his feet sending his chair crashing to the floor. He scurried to the door not wanting to incur the wrath of Diaz for he knew that that could have unpleasant consequences.

Diaz looked at Jim and a grin broke the bags of flesh which hung from his jowl. 'Come, Senor Jim, don't look so angry. You and I are friends. Haven't we both kept the bargain made when you came here?' He spread his hands in a gesture of pleading to be understood, and raised one thick, bushy eyebrow quizzically as he put the question.

'Sure,' agreed Jim, 'but I don't supply you with my surplus mustangs to ride this side of the Rio Grande.'

'Aw, just now and again, Jim,' Diaz put on a hurt look at the inference he read behind Jim's words.

'Quit stalling, Diaz,' rapped Jim with some annoyance. 'Get down to it. What do you want me for?'

'Sit down, Jim, and we'll talk. Maybe that pretty lady of yours will give us another cup of coffee.'

Jim glanced at his wife and with an almost

imperceptible nod of his head showed his approval of Diaz's suggestion. He picked up the chair which had been knocked over and lowered his strong, muscular body on to it.

'Well?' he prompted, eyeing Diaz coolly as the Mexican slid his hand inside the open front of his worn shirt and scratched his hairy chest vigorously.

'Ah, zat is better,' grinned Diaz, leaning back on his chair. 'It is not a pleasant story I have to tell you, Jim. Maybe…' There was no need to express his meaning in words as he glanced towards Kate.

She caught that glance as she turned to the table with the coffee-pot. 'Nothing would shock me after the filthy talk of yon two last night,' rapped Kate as she stared down contemptuously at the Mexican.

Diaz's glance at Jim was troubled. He shrugged his shoulders as he said, 'I cannot stop my men from talking.'

Jim's eyes narrowed and his lips tightened. Diaz read the signs and he knew that this was no time to toy with Jim Hooper. The ex-lawman may have slowed a little but he was still mighty handy with a gun and Diaz had no illusions as to who would come off best if it ever came to a straight gunfight. Diaz needed cunning and men to back him up, but even though he knew he could out-play Jim in this way he had thought it wisest to play along with Jim's suggestion of friendly arrangements when the Hoopers had decided to settle close to the Rio Grande.

'You want to stay?' Jim strengthened his query with concern in his eyes.

'I'll stay,' replied Kate, smoothing her dark hair back from her forehead. As their eyes locked, Jim knew she wanted to share this as they had shared so much of life together. She wanted to know why Diaz wanted Jim, for trouble for Jim was also trouble for her.

Jim nodded and as Kate poured the coffee he watched her closely. He counted himself fortunate to have had Kate to share his life. There were times when it could not have been easy for her. Life with a lawman was no easy thing, especially as he could be a target for killing. He had seen the worry begin to age her and line the smoothness of her skin, detracting from the beauty he carried with him wherever he went. So it was that he had agreed to give up his job as sheriff of Rosewell County and when he saw the worry lifted from Kate, making her ten years younger, he regretted he had not done it before. Now some of those years had come back and he did not want them.

When Kate had finished pouring the coffee, Jim diverted his gaze to Diaz and the Mexican did not lose one more moment before starting his story.

'It concerns my brother, Senor Jim. Three gringos kill him.'

Although he showed no reaction to the news, Jim was surprised, for Carlos Diaz was so different to his brother. A small, mild-mannered man, he lived close to his brother but took no part in the bandit ways of the older man.

'So?' prompted Jim casually.

Diaz's eyes flashed. 'My brother is dead,

Jim. Three gringos torture and kill him.'

'What has this to do with me?' asked Jim with some irritation as Diaz paused again.

'They cross the border. You know I can't follow them. I want you to get them for me! Bring them to me alive.' As he had been speaking Diaz had moved his hand stealthily to the pistol nestling in the leather beside his thigh.

'But I...' The words froze on Jim's lips when he saw the muzzle of a pistol pointing at him across the table. Anger smouldered in his narrowing eyes.

'No buts, Senor Jim. You will do as I say because I am going to take your wife with me, a hostage to make sure you bring those men back to me alive!'

Alarm and fear flared in Kate's eyes as she swung round from the table near the door where she had been washing the dirty plates.

'Like hell you will!' hissed Jim stiffening in his chair.

'Like hell I WILL,' Diaz's grin revealed not only a row of broken yellow-stained

17

teeth but also his pleasure in the power his pistol gave him. 'This gun is trained on your belly. There'll be one big mess if I have to pull the trigger.'

Kate gave Jim a pleading look to do nothing rash as she came to his side. He took her hand in his, trying to comfort the alarm which he knew must be tearing through his wife.

'How the hell do you expect me to be able to track them down?' protested Jim.

'You have a reputation, Senor Jim. You'll find them.'

'But I don't know where to start. I don't even know what they look like.'

'Ah, I will tell you. Carlos was not dead when I found him. He was able to tell me. Now I will tell you. One was a tall, thin man. His face was hollow, his eyes they were sunk. Carlos say they were cold eyes, showed nothing except pleasure when he castrated him and cut off...' Diaz hesitated and shot Kate a glance. 'I told you this wouldn't be pleasant.'

'Go on,' pressed Jim. 'The others.'

'Another was ... how you say it? ... middle build but strong. Dark, almost black hair and he dressed in black. Long scar, maybe knife wound, down his right cheek.'

Jim felt Kate's grip tighten as she sank on to a chair beside him. A quick glance told him she had recognised the men. Her face had drained of its colour and he knew her fear was for his safety and not for her own.

'The third?' asked Jim quietly, knowing the answer before it came.

'Short, stocky, hard. His face ... how you say? ... bust up, been in fights. That is what he like, punch Carlos bad before thin man work on him. They hung Carlos by his thumbs and work on him.' Diaz's eyes burned with a deep hate. 'He was not a nice sight when I found him. The knife had been used to torture and maim. He was cut deep at the back of the heels. He... Maybe it was better he die.' Diaz looked hard at Jim. 'You find them, bring them to me, I Fernandez Diaz will deal with them.'

'Jim they...' started Kate but the sudden pressure of Jim's hand silenced her.

'That gun tells me I must do it,' put in Jim quickly.

'That's right, Jim,' grinned Diaz. 'You talk sensible.'

'But you listen to this Diaz,' went on Jim, his gaze boring into the Mexican, leaving him in no doubt as to the consequences if he did not heed his words. 'You let anyone harm my wife in any way I'll kill you as well as them.'

'You need not worry, Senor Jim. Your wife will be perfectly safe with me.'

'She'd better be. Now I want a word with her alone.'

'Ah, you expect me to go?' said Diaz, slowly shaking his head.

'Alone!'

Diaz hesitated for a moment but seeing the determination on Jim's face he agreed. 'I'll take your gun.' He watched Jim carefully as the ex-lawman eased his Colt from its holster and handed it butt-first to the Mexican.

Diaz stood up and walked to the door. 'Only a few moments.'

'Jim!' cried Kate as the door closed. 'You know who they are?' Anxiety creased her face dragging back that age which Jim had been glad to see lifted when they had come to the Rio Grande.

'Of course,' Jim tried to sound casual about it. 'Crazy Joe Reed, Blackie Fallon and Fist Parker.'

'They threatened to kill you when they got out of gaol.'

'Words.' Jim hoped he sounded convincing.

'Then what are they doing down here?' asked Kate, her anxiety driven deeper by Jim's apparent casualness.

'That's just what I'd like to know,' mused Jim. 'They're out before their time. Maybe broke gaol. But why go south of the border and come back where they're more than likely still wanted men? Why kill Carlos? You know the money from the bank robbery was never found.'

Kate grabbed her husband by the arms. She did not like the look which had come to his face. She had seen it before whenever Jim had sensed a hunt and she had known nothing but a bullet would stop him reaching the end of that particular trail. 'Jim!' she cried. 'You can't!' Tears welled in the eyes which pleaded.

'Kate, I must. Diaz has me in a corner.'

'Tell him who they are. What they threatened. He wouldn't make you go then.'

'It would make no difference to him. All he wants is revenge for what they did to his brother.' He looked deep into his wife's tear-filled eyes. 'I've got to do it. Don't let Diaz know that I know these men. There's something strange about this whole thing.'

All further talk was stopped as the door was flung open with a crash. Extra light flooded into the room only to almost disappear again as Diaz's bulky body filled the doorway.

'Enough,' he boomed. 'Time to go.'

As they stood up Kate flung herself against

Jim. He held her tight as he whispered, 'I love you. I'll be back as soon as I can. I'll be all right.'

Kate clung as he tried to ease her away.

'Go, my darling. Don't anger Diaz. It's best if we play along with him.'

Kate nodded. Biting her lip, trying to hold back the tears, she turned reluctantly away and walked hesitantly to the door.

'My men have saddled your horse,' said Diaz as he stepped to one side to allow Kate to pass. 'Your gun, Senor Jim.' He tossed Jim's Colt on to the floor. 'Remember I want them alive.' His eyes held Jim's for a brief moment before he turned and strode to his horse.

Jim watched him mount, picked up his gun and went to the door. He knew he could easily drop the three Mexicans but he had never shot a man without facing him. Even if he did kill the three Mexicans his situation would be little better. Reed, Fallon and Parker had threatened him and he read it as no idle threat. One day they would

come hunting. Was this the time? But crossing the border and killing Carlos Diaz did
not fit the pattern. Far better for him to
start the hunt, better to be the hunter rather
than the hunted. This way they could not
use Kate to get at him. In Diaz's camp she
would be safe from them.

Jim shoved his Colt back into its holster,
waved to his wife and watched them ride
away, before preparing for the hunt.

TWO

Jim prepared for his departure quickly but methodically. There was no point in wasting time for the sooner he cleared up this matter the sooner he and Kate could resume their life. If indeed he was able to run it to a successful conclusion. Jim knew these three men, knew their ruthless cunning and he had no illusions about the task which faced him. It was one thing finding them, and that would not be easy, but it was another getting the three of them back alive to Diaz.

Once he had tidied things up to his liking, he packed sufficient food to see him through the rest of the day and disposed of the remainder. It was no use leaving any in the house for he had no way of knowing how long he would be away. He knew Diaz would keep an eye on his property and his horses so after turning three of them into the corral he saddled the mount he had chosen for its strength.

The jet-black horse had been leader of a herd which Jim had seen shortly after coming to the Rio Grande. He had been struck by the pride in the lift of its head, and by the spirited fire in its eyes. Its broad deep chest betrayed a powerhouse of energy which drove it into a motion which filled Jim with a bottomless admiration. Jim had never seen anything more beautiful than the black at full gallop. He had determined then that one day the horse would be his but it had taken him six months before he cornered the proud animal. It had been a contest which in some ways Jim was sorry had come to an end.

The respect which man and horse had for each other soon turned into a deeper understanding and love. Midnight, as Kate had called it immediately on seeing the horse, nuzzled Jim as they walked to the house. He patted the smooth neck, gleaming under the

Texan sun, 'We'll soon have Kate back, you and I,' he muttered with a determination which the horse sensed.

Jim secured his bedroll and slicker to his saddle, stowed his food and extra ammunition, and saw that he had a canteen full of water. He checked his Winchester 44, a weapon which he did not normally carry when mustanging. Satisfied, he slipped it into the doeskin scabbard which he favoured and secured it to the saddle horn. His face was grim as he examined his short-barrel Colt Peacemaker .45 with a cut away trigger guard, for he knew this was the weapon which might keep him alive if he caught up with the men he hunted. He slipped it back into its leather holster, the toe of which was held firmly to his thigh by a thin leather thong. After adjusting the feel of his gun-belt he slid the Peacemaker into his hand, feeling his fingers mould to the weapon. He replaced the revolver in its holster and then, in a movement which almost defied the eye, the gun was back in his hand, the finger curled around the trigger. His body was tense, his eyes concentrated on a spot about twenty yards in front of him. As he relaxed and slipped the Colt back into the leather he grunted with satisfaction.

He was pleased with his movement and the speed of his draw. Maybe he was a shade slower than in his younger days but he was still fast.

Jim took one last look around the house, locked it and rode up the slope without a backward glance. He knew if he had done so too many happy memories of a peaceful life with Kate would flood his mind and divert it from the task ahead, a task he knew would require all his undivided attention and cool reasoning if he was to succeed and be able to return to the life he wanted.

Once he had gained the ridge he turned Midnight in a south-easterly direction following the Rio Grande towards the only location clue he had. He frowned as he thought of the thinness of that clue– Diaz had told him the men had been seen crossing the Rio Grande and though that could have been in several places along the river the crossing nearest to Diaz's territory was close to Bosque Bonito. It was a crossing likely to be taken by men in a hurry to leave Diaz's territory and the three bank robbers would be in a big hurry if Diaz was on their trail.

Jim kept his horse to a leisurely pace. As much as the desire burned in him to press on with all haste, to find these men, return and release Kate, he knew it would be foolish to overtax his horse and himself. There could be a lot of riding ahead. The three men could be anywhere.

He puzzled over their presence in this part of the country. He presumed they had escaped from gaol, their sentences still had a considerable time to run, so it would have been natural for them to make for the border, but why return?

They had threatened to hunt him down when they got out of gaol but if that was their reason for being in this part of Texas why had they crossed the border into

Mexico? Why run foul of Fernandez Diaz, cruel, ruthless, autocratic ruler of a large slice of territory along the border? Why murder Carlos Diaz and run the risk of a terrifying revenge?

Jim was no nearer finding a solution to any of the questions when he slowed his horse to a halt on the slope to the crossing of the Rio Grande. No-one rode the dusty trail which continued beyond the steadily flowing river in a south-easterly direction towards the small collection of adobe buildings grouped haphazardly about a mile away.

From the shielding brim of his stetson his eyes beat at the distance but the only movement he saw was caused by the shimmering heat reflected from the arid land. The town, if such a God-forsaken place could be graced with such a term, moved in a dance of mockery as if it knew the enormity of his task.

A heavy weight of depression overwhelmed him. He was a hunter again, a hunter of men, something from which he thought he had escaped three years ago. That life had vanished but now it was back and Jim did not want it. All he wanted was the peaceful life with Kate.

Midnight snorted and shook his head startling Jim out of the apathy which had threatened him. He straightened in the saddle, squared his shoulders and frowned with annoyance at himself for allowing despair to take over.

He was the hunter again. He was the man who would only be stopped by a bullet.

Jim licked at his dried lips and reached for his canteen. He stopped as his hand closed around it. 'Save it. You'll get a drink in Bosque Bonito,' he muttered.

Tapping his horse forward he eased slowly down the slope towards the river. Midnight needed no cajoling into the water and Jim slipped from the saddle to revel in the Rio Grande's coolness. Both horse and man welcomed its salving effect as it ridded them of the dust of the trail.

The sun beating fiercely from a cloudless

sky soon dried them out as they headed for the group of buildings, most of which were in some need of repair. It looked even more dilapidated than it did when Jim had visited it shortly after he and Kate had come to the south-west. Looking for possible markets for his mustangs he had not found one in Bosque Bonito. He had realised this almost as soon as he had reached the place so a brief word and one quick drink and then he was on his way. He guessed, now, no-one would remember him.

The street bore little resemblance to one, with buildings placed at any old angle except for two small groups which had been sited in some sort of symmetry. It was towards one of these groups that Jim rode. No-one was on the street but Jim felt eyes watching him. No doubt their owners were thinking 'only mad gringos move in this heat'.

Jim swung from the saddle in front of a low building which had the word *cantina* scrawled in black paint on a piece of board nailed to the wall beside an opening in which a door hung drunkenly on its hinges. Openings at head height on either side of the door acted as windows which could be covered if necessary by the hessian now tied back.

Jim eyed the broken awning and, deciding its spasmodic covering was better than none, he led his horse under it and tied it to a metal ring in the wall. If he gained no more than on his last visit he would soon be riding out of Bosque Bonito.

Stepping into the cantina, Jim paused to let his eyes adjust to what was gloom after the glare of the high sun. When his eyes became accustomed to the new light he saw that all the occupants of the room were staring at him. They presented a tableau as if his entry had frozen them into immobility. About twelve peons sat or sprawled against tables around the room, wilting under the oppressive heat and the stench of human sweat. Two girls sat on stools against the wooden erection which served as a bar. The thin one tried to rival her more buxom partner's display by a greater show of leg but both their efforts were lost on the occupants of the room for they had seen it all before.

The girls were the first to move, straightening on their stools, sending life pulsating through their bodies and adjusting their dress to provoke the man who stood in the doorway and in whom they saw more prospects than in the peons who littered the room.

As he stepped forward Jim saw the two girls shoot an enquiring glance at the huge man who leaned heavily on the counter. His dark eyes sunk in folds of flesh had never left Jim but Jim knew he had been aware of the girls' glances for Jim noted an almost imperceptible nod in reply, in fact Jim realised if he had not been studying the man he would have missed it. But Jim had seen it and sharpened his senses to be on guard against any collusion between the three people at the counter.

'Good day, senor.' The man's voice growled from the depths of his chest and his pendulous jowls wobbled with the words.

As hot as it was outside Jim felt it would be more welcome than the stench in the room but he needed information if it was here. However he was nearly driven to leaving when he neared the counter for the smell which came from the man was nauseating. His shirt must have forgotten the day it was white. It was open to the top of his trousers revelling a dense, hairy chest and huge stomach which hung over the top of his trousers. His black, matted hair had probably not felt water from the day he was born. Sweat formed in droplets on his heavily-lined brow and ran, now and again, in tiny rivulets down his face to be brushed away by fat fingers.

Jim nodded in reply. 'Beer.'

'No beer, senor,' returned the man. 'Only whisky.'

'But...' started Jim.

'Only whisky,' growled the man behind the counter with a take-it-or-leave-it attitude.

Jim knew there would be beer of sorts somewhere for those peons who did have a glass were not using that size for whisky. He halted the words of protest which came to his lips. He wanted information not argument from this oversized barman.

'Whisky,' Jim nodded.

The man shuffled his huge frame round and reached for a bottle on a shelf on the wall behind the counter. His bulk blocked Jim's view of his actions as he poured the drink.

'You ridden far, senor? Maybe you tired of the trail and want nice place to rest, nice pleasures to take your mind off your troubles.' The voice was soft and caressing, drawing away something of the unpleasant atmosphere of this run-down cantina in a place rotting in the dregs of time.

As Jim turned his head to reply to the buxom girl he was just in time to see her sharp glance return from the movements of the man pouring his drink.

'I've ridden far. I'm tired but what I want is

36

information.' He was amused by the sudden extinguishing of the eager light which had sprung to the girl's eyes with his first words.

'Maybe you don't like it too easy.' A new hope had come to the girl who slid from her stool and came to one beside Jim.

'What about your friend?' queried Jim with a slight inclination of his head in the direction of the thinner girl whose eyes had flashed annoyance at the other taking the initiative.

'Ah,' there was a touch of derision in the girl's voice. 'Chiquita, she no good, too thin. Now me, Rosita, I have more. I give you a good time. Pedro will tell you.'

'We'll see,' replied Jim. 'It's information I want first.'

'Information, senor?' said the fat man as he turned from the shelf with Jim's drink which he thrust on to the counter. 'What information would we have in a poor place like this?' His air of innocence amused Jim.

'Maybe a lot. You see people come, you see people go. You see people cross the river,' replied Jim.

'We are a quiet town, senor,' said Pedro.

Jim ignored the barman's comment and glanced at Rosita. He shoved his drink to her. 'Have this one,' he offered, 'I'll get another.'

'No. It's all right. It is yours.' Rosita pushed the glass back at Jim, who noted her haste and the touch of alarm in her voice. 'Pedro will get me one.'

The fat man was quick to respond and had a glass and bottle in his hands before Jim could reply.

'If you are a quiet town,' Jim said, meeting Pedro's dark stare, 'you would remember strangers.'

'Maybe.'

'If you don't, maybe the girls do,' returned Jim with a quick glance at Rosita and Chiquita. 'Three men, Americans. One very dark, scar down right cheek, another tall and thin and the third stocky, face marked with fighting.'

The warning glance from Pedro to the two girls was so slight that, coming from eyes almost hidden by rolls of flesh, Jim almost missed it.

'Ah, I remember now,' said Pedro with a smile which as it split the heavy jowls revealed a row of yellow-stained teeth. 'You, you are the man who tries to sell mustangs, the ex-lawman who lives along the Rio Grande.' He took pleasure in his knowledge as he stared hard at Jim. 'You back with the law? Mustanging does not pay?'

'No business of yours,' retorted Jim sharply. 'Do you remember these men?'

'No, senor, I don't. They not come here.'

'What about you two girls, you see them?' asked Jim glancing from one to the other.

'No,' replied Rosita with a shrug of her shoulders.

Chiquita shook her head but Jim felt there was something not quite convincing in the look in her eyes. For a moment Jim was about to press her but decided that with the presence of the huge Pedro she would be afraid to say anything.

'Ah, well, I'll have to try elsewhere,' said

Jim resignedly. He toyed thoughtfully with his glass without raising it to his lips.

'You drink, senor. Then I make you forget these men until morning.'

'I'll drink, but not that!' Jim's words came with such a snap that they startled Rosita. 'You drink it!'

'No, senor. It is yours. I have mine.' There was a touch of alarm in Rosita's voice which matched the sudden concern in her eyes.

'Drink it!' Jim's voice had gone cold, menacing.

'No, senor, no!' Rosita's eyes widened under Jim's threatening gaze.

'Senor, please, no trouble,' Pedro put in his plea weakly. It was as Jim had judged. Pedro relied on his huge bulk to frighten people. With it came an overpowering attitude but there was nothing behind it. Pedro had no spunk when it came to a showdown.

'Drink!'

Rosita hesitated. Like a snake striking, Jim's hand snatched. His thumb and forefingers closed on her nose and at the same time forced her head backwards, her mouth opened as she gasped for breath and in that moment Jim swept up the glass and poured its contents into her mouth. He clamped her jaw shut and all Rosita could do was swallow. Satisfied that the liquid had all gone, Jim released her.

'You goddamned gringo!' Rosita trembled with rage. Her dark eyes blazed with an angry fire and her long fingers curled claw-like as she crouched, facing Jim. 'I'll rip your eyes out!'

She sprang but Jim was ready for her. She found she could not get beyond the strong hand which held her at arm's length, turned her and pushed her hard against the bar. She clawed and kicked but her efforts only cut through the air.

'You'll sleep long tonight, Rosita,' laughed Jim. 'What were you going to do? You and Pedro fleece me? Maybe dump my body in the Rio Grande?'

'Me, senor?' protested Pedro innocently.

'Yes, you,' snarled Jim, disgusted that such

a man had not moved one finger to help Rosita. 'Laced my drink when it was hidden by that fat belly.'

Rosita's struggles were subsiding. Jim slackened his grip. 'You going to behave now?' he asked quietly. A glazed look was coming to her eyes and Jim released his hold. As she leaned against the bar her legs began to buckle. 'Help her,' Jim snapped at Pedro and the huge man gripped Rosita over the counter and at the same time with an inclination of his head signed for help from some of the peons who had remained unconcerned throughout the whole incident, too frightened to interfere.

As three of them hurried forward Jim turned from the bar and started towards the door. His step hesitated against Chiquita. 'Rosita said you too thin, no good for a man.' He deliberately kept his voice low.

Chiquita tossed her head, her eyes flashing contempt in the direction of Rosita. 'She no good now.' There was a flicker of amusement in her eyes as they met Jim's.

'I'll camp by the ford tonight,' he whispered and continued on his way out of the cantina.

THREE

Jim tensed, his whole being alerted by the faint sound coming out of the darkness which lay on the land on each side of the Rio Grande.

He nipped out his cheroot and inclined his head, listening intently. Nothing, only the usual night sounds of the arid land. No, there it was again, a quiet rustle and then silence, a movement and then stillness. It came again, a little louder, nearer.

Jim rose silently from his reclining position in the slight hollow near the ford and crouched with gun drawn.

The sound, never loud, came nearer and the movement became continuous. Now Jim was certain someone was approaching his night camp. His ears, now attuned to it, recognised a lightness so that when there was a pause he was not surprised to hear a female voice whisper, 'Senor? Senor?'

Jim slipped his gun back into its holster and straightened as he called, 'Over here.' His voice was low but penetrating and as he moved out of the hollow he saw a form rise from the ground where it had been crouching and run towards him.

'Senor, I'm so glad I found you,' gasped Chiquita when she reached Jim who guided her back into the hollow.

'I thought you might come,' he said keeping his voice low.

'And I think you not want me for myself,' returned Chiquita as she pulled her shawl more tightly around her thin shoulders.

'You are right,' replied Jim, a note of apology in his voice. 'I'm sorry.'

'So am I,' said Chiquita. 'You would have been nice after that beast who was here a few days ago.' The gentle tone of regret had suddenly changed to venomous hate.

'So there were some men at Bosque Bonito recently?' Jim pressed excitedly. 'I thought there might have been. I figured Pedro was lying and I reckoned you might be the one who would help me.'

'Si, senor, I can. It may not be much, even if they are the same men you seek.'

'Anything will help,' went on Jim, eager for any information no matter how slim. 'I need to find them and all I know is that they crossed the Rio, back into Texas maybe three days ago.'

Chiquita's face showed some disappointment. 'Maybe they are not the same, senor; these men went further into Mexico.'

'But they could have come back,' pressed Jim. 'Three of them. Did they fit the description I gave in the cantina?'

'That was not very much to go on,' Chiquita pointed out quietly.

'Sufficient to recognise them,' snapped Jim, annoyed at the hesitancy in Chiquita. He grabbed her by the shoulders and stared hard at her. 'It's vital I know. If one of them treated you badly you'd recognise him even from my brief description.' Suspicion filled

Jim as Chiquita pouted. 'What is it you want? Why are you holding back on me?'

'Senor, those men are bad. They threaten. The tall, thin one with cold sunken eyes, he treat me bad, made me do things I not like and then he torture me for his own pleasure.' An icy hate had come to Chiquita's voice. 'Revenge,' she hissed. 'I want him dead!'

'Then tell me,' urged Jim.

'But, senor, if I speak I don't know if you will succeed and if you don't and those men return knowing someone spoke...' She shuddered, not wanting to contemplate the horrors she imagined would befall her. 'If I speak I cannot go back to the cantina.'

Jim released his grip on her shoulders. So that was it. She wanted to get away, wanted him to help her escape the hopeless existence in Bosque Bonito. But where could he take her? What could he do with her? He was a hunter on the trail of dangerous men and he wanted no hindrances. But he wanted information, no matter how slight, and he would have to make a promise to get it and he was not a man to break a promise.

'Look, Chiquita, maybe I have to ride far after you speak. I'll come back for you.'

The light of hope vanished from Chiquita's eyes to be replaced by one of fear. 'Senor, I cannot go back, you must take me with you. You want information, you take me.' She grabbed Jim's arm. 'You must!'

Jim stared into the dark pools of fear for a moment, then nodded slowly. 'All right,' he said quietly.

'You promise, senor?' She gazed in wide-eyed desperation at him.

'Yes, I promise,' he said with a look which brought reassurance to the girl. 'Now tell me what you know.'

'They came into the cantina about a week ago. They look as if they had ridden far.'

'Did they say where they had come from?' interrupted Jim.

'No. They told Pedro not to be nosey when he asked. Then one of them must have made some joke for they all laughed.'

'What did he say?'

'Something about Pedro would lose his belly where they had come from. And then another said he'd need to do what they had done.'

'Nothing else about that?' asked Jim when Chiquita hesitated.

'No.' Chiquita shook her head.

Jim nodded thoughtfully. More than likely they were referring to prison where the work and diet would certainly take some fat off Pedro. 'To do what they had done' Jim pondered. Probably escaped by squeezing through a narrow opening where Pedro's belly would have stopped him.

'What else?' pressed Jim, for so far this information was of little use to him. 'Did they say where they were going or why they had come to Mexico?'

'No, but they ask Pedro if he know a Carlos Diaz.'

'And did he?' urged Jim, a note of excitement in his voice.

'Yes, he tell them he is the brother of the

bandit Fernandez Diaz.'

'Were they surprised at this?'

Chiquita frowned thoughtfully. 'Si, I think so. They look at each other and then ask Pedro if he knew where they could find Carlos Diaz.'

'And did Pedro know?'

'Si, he know but he reluctant to tell. I suppose he afraid of Fernandez but these men were in the cantina and they threaten. They demonstrate on some poor peon what they would do to Pedro if he did not tell them. It was not pretty and Pedro tell them how to find Fernandez for where he lives there is Carlos.'

'Did they say why they wanted Carlos?'

'No, senor.'

'They left then to find Carlos?' prompted Jim.

'They not leave till next morning. It was not a pleasant night.' Chiquita shuddered at the memory.

'The man who was with you, did…'

Chiquita broke in with a grunt of disgust.

'Beast!' She spat and uttered a curse on his head.

'Did he say anything while in your company which might help me?' went on Jim, ignoring the interruption.

'No, senor, no. He talk nothing about himself except to make a promise I hope he never keeps.'

'What was that?' Jim asked automatically as disappointment at the paucity of the information began to seize him.

'He promised he'd be back one day with plenty of money and he'd pay me well to entertain him again.'

Jim's growing disappointment vanished as the words bit into his mind. He hadn't received any information as to the whereabouts of the three men but could this casual remark be a clue as to their purpose in coming to Mexico to seek out Carlos Diaz? The only way Crazy Joe Reed was likely to get rich was through the recovery and split of the bank robbery money. Was that why they had come to Mexico? Was that why they wanted Carlos? Could Carlos be the fourth man? If not, why look for him? If not, what other connection was there? And why kill him?

The questions tumbled in Jim's mind and with them a multitude of answers but one thing kept troubling him; he could not picture Carlos as a bank robber, he was too retiring, too inconspicuous and yet Jim had to admit to himself that outward appearances could be deceiving. The fourth man had never been identified and it had always been assumed he had been an American. Now Jim began to wonder if he could have been a Mexican.

'Has that been of help, senor?' Chiquita broke into Jim's thoughts.

'Possibly,' he replied. 'We must talk some more, there may be something else. But we can do that as we ride.'

'You take me, senor? You take me?' There was excited delight in Chiquita's voice and eyes.

'I promised,' said Jim and set about preparing to leave. In a few moments all was ready and once he had the girl behind him on the horse he turned Midnight to the ford and they were soon back on Texas soil.

'Where are you taking me, senor?' queried Chiquita.

'I'll take you to my house. My wife is away. You can stay there until I return.'

'What if she come back before you?'

'She won't. Now, can you tell me anything else?'

'No I don't think so.'

'Did they come back to Bosque Bonito?'

'No, but I saw them.'

'You saw them?' Jim could not hide his surprise.

'Yes, senor. From a distance two days ago. They ride quickly and cross the Rio Grande without coming to Bosque Bonito.'

'You saw them close?'

'No, senor. I said from a distance and I mean long way off.'

'But how could you be certain it was them?'

'When they left to look for Carlos I watch

them ride away with hate and fear in my heart. The way they rode I remember so that if they came back I would know them from a long way off.'

'And then you could hide,' added Jim.

'Si, senor. I want no more to do with them.'

'Not even if Crazy Joe Reed came back rich?'

'No!' The word spat from between tight-drawn lips.

'So they crossed the river. Did you see which way they went once they were on this side?'

'They turn this way.'

'The way we are riding now?'

'Si, senor.'

Jim was puzzled. Riding in this direction might indicate that they were on a revenge ride to kill him as they had sworn. But he had not seen any sign of them. They could have turned anywhere once out of Chiquita's sight and she would not know.

'Think hard, Chiquita. Did you ever hear any other place mentioned?'

'No,' Chiquita drew the word out thought-fully.

'What happened the morning they left?'

'They had breakfast and went.'

'Who served them with breakfast?'

'Me and Rosita.'

'Did you hear anything while you were serving?'

'I did not stay. I push the plates in front of them and get away from their pawing hands quick. I remember the night too much.'

'The odd word, Chiquita, surely you heard the odd word? Think! As you were coming and going, didn't anything reach your ears?'

Chiquita paused for a moment thought-fully then said tentatively, 'Well one mentioned a rose and a well.'

'A rose? Strange thing for the likes of Crazy Joe Reed to talk about.'

'I heard one say something about a field, a green one I think. Oh, yes, now I remember, a wood and a lake. And they mentioned Carl.'

'Carl? No other name?' pressed Jim as he puzzled over the improbability of a conversation concerning nature from Crazy Joe Reed, Blackie Fallon and Fist Parker. It was laughable, so much so that Jim almost missed Chiquita's reply.

'No, they did not give him another name but they did say he was bad.'

'Bad?'

'Yes.'

'You sure it wasn't Carlos?'

'Si, I'm sure. It was Carl. They said Carl's bad.'

'Carl's bad?' Jim savoured the words trying to recall anyone by the name of Carl who might be associated with the three men, 'Carl's bad?' Suddenly the true meaning struck him forcibly. 'Carlsbad, not Carl's bad! It's the name of a place on the Pecos!' Excitement rose in Jim's voice as his mind raced over the rest of the information.

'You know it?'

'Sure. You said field and green that'll be Greenfield, and there's Lakewood and Rosewell. All places on the Pecos!' Excitement surged through Jim. Rosewell, his own territory when he had been sheriff; Rosewell, where the bank robbery had taken place. The trail of the robbers had led him along the Rio Hondo and he had caught up with them in Sunset. It had been generally assumed that the fourth man, who had escaped, had been with his three partners and when he had evaded capture that he had continued west. His trail had not been picked up.

Now Jim's mind was racing with another possibility not considered at the time. Supposing the fourth man had never been with his three companions along the Rio Hondo; supposing they acted as decoys, while he headed south along the Pecos, they hoping to avoid capture and rejoin him later. The perfect getaway.

They had mentioned Rosewell, Greenfield, Lakewood and Carlsbad in the cantina, could these names be significant? Could this be the way the fourth man had ridden, maybe to a prearranged route? And if that fourth man was Carlos it would be the natural route for him to take before diverting to Mexico. But did the names signify that the three men had headed there after their interview with Carlos? How could they? Hadn't the names been heard before they contacted Carlos? No matter, they could have been discussing possibilities to clear up with Carlos. In any case they were the only leads he had and so must be the ones he had to follow.

FOUR

'Chiquita, you are to stay here until I get back. Keep the place clean and tidy. It will be better with someone living in it. I have written a note saying who you are and that you have my permission to be here. Show it to anyone who comes and questions you. It may be Fernandez Diaz or his men.'

Alarm showed on Chiquita's face as she faced Jim across the table in Jim's house. They had camped for the night once Jim was satisfied that no-one from the cantina would find them. Once they had reached the house the following morning Jim lost no time in settling Chiquita and was now preparing to leave.

'There's no need to be frightened of Fernandez or his men,' went on Jim quickly to reassure her. 'I have an understanding with him and he knows what will happen to him if he goes against me. So you'll be all right.'

There were grateful tears in Chiquita's eyes as she bade him goodbye and watched him ride away. His were the first kindnesses she could remember.

Jim did not look back as he topped the rise. The sight of the house and the girl would have stirred up too many memories of Kate and he felt he did not want to see the house again until he returned with her.

Once over the ridge, Jim turned his horse to move parallel to the Rio Grande in the direction of El Paso. His thoughts turned to the information he had gleaned from Chiquita and he became more convinced that the men he sought had been referring to towns along the Pecos.

Jim felt sure he would find the answers he sought by the waters of the Pecos. But would the three men return to an area where they must be remembered? After all it was only three years since they robbed the bank in Rosewell. Memory of that had not had time to fade, especially as the money had never been recovered and the talk of a fourth man occupied a prominent part of the theories of the robbery. All of which must have been brought sharply back to the communities along the Pecos when the news of the gaolbreak had broken. The law, bounty-hunters and those hoping to be led to a rich haul would all be on the look out for the three gaolbreakers.

Under these conditions it would have to be some very strong reason to get them to return to Rosewell and the Pecos especially as they had successfully evaded the law and had reached Mexico. There had to be a very good reason for them to throw up freedom and risk recapture by recrossing the Rio Grande. Jim figured that the only reason strong enough was money and that that money had to be from the bank in Rosewell.

The more he thought about the matter the more it seemed that Carlos, if he was the fourth man, had not taken the money, or certainly not all of it, to Mexico. If he had why should the other three return to a land where they were hunted men? Had they made Carlos talk before he died? If so they would collect it as soon as possible and get clear of the region. Even now he might be too late to pick up their trail.

But what of himself? What of the threat they had made to hunt him down and kill him? They could not know his whereabouts otherwise they would not have missed the chance when they were so close on the Rio Grande, even though the bank money would be uppermost in their minds. But once that was recovered Jim had no illusions that he would be their next target. They were killers. He must play his cards right and keep the advantage he had of being the hunter. And Jim figured the best place to start would be the scene of the crime, Rosewell.

Eight days later, the dust of long travel hanging on man and horse, Jim stopped Midnight in front of the sheriff's office in Rosewell. He knew his slow ride along the main street had attracted the attention of the few men who lounged on the sidewalk seeking the protection of its awning from the hot sun. He knew it would not be long before the whole town knew Jim Hooper was back.

He eyed the wooden building as he swung from the saddle. Nothing had changed since he left except that the notice board carried a wanted notice for Crazy Joe Reed, Blackie Fallon and Fist Parker. It stated 'Dead or Alive' and Jim was reminded that he had a problem on his hands. He wanted them alive whereas anyone else would shoot first and ask questions later. He had to beat everyone else to the gaolbreakers and then he had to keep them alive until he reached Diaz.

He stepped on to the sidewalk, rapped on the office door and walked in.

'Jim Hooper!' The sheriff gasped when he looked up from the papers on his desk. His rugged, weatherbeaten face broke into a welcoming smile as he pushed himself to his feet and came from behind his desk. 'It's great to see you.' He took Jim's hand in a firm grip.

'You too,' grinned Jim. 'How've you been, Clem?' he added, recalling the gangly eighteen-year-old he had taken on as deputy fifteen years ago.

'Fine, just fine,' replied Clem. 'What brings you back here, thought you said you'd never be back? How's Kate?' There seemed to be so much that Clem wanted to know that the questions began to pour off his lips but he pulled himself up short and a look of concern crossed his face. 'Hi, you know Crazy Joe Reed and his sidekicks broke gaol?'

'Yeah, I know,' replied Jim, his face grim, 'and they're linked with your other questions.'

Alarmed incredulity sparked in Clem's deep brown eyes. 'Kate! Not Kate?'

'She's all right,' Jim hastened to reassure his friend, though the gravity in his face did not change. Jim went on to tell Clem his story, only pausing to accept the whisky

Clem produced from his desk.

When Jim had finished Clem let out a low whistle. 'You sure are in a tight spot. There's a poster out on those men.'

'Yeah, saw it as I came in.'

'Dead or alive,' Clem pointed out.

'I noticed,' said Jim grimly.

'Then you've sure got to find them hombres quick or Diaz may only get dead men.'

'Right,' agreed Jim. 'So I'm here. Anything you can tell me which might help?'

'Little,' replied Clem. 'They made the break, killing a guard in the escape. Next report was of three horses and saddles stolen from a ranch. Only one other which may or may not have been connected. Three men were seen south of Hope on the Rio Penasco heading up into the Sacramentos. Since then nothing until you walk in. And you can't be sure they're back up this way.'

'No, but I've got to play the only leads I have no matter how thin. No reports from Carlsbad, Lakewood or Greenfield?'

'Nothing,' answered Clem. 'Wish there were. But your supposition that they were referring to those places is pretty thin. Remember we felt certain that there was a fourth man and that he got away when we took Reed, Fallon and Parker and that he'd headed further into the mountains. If it was Carlos as you imply he could have crossed right over to Tularosa and then headed south to El Paso and from there into Mexico and to his brother.'

'Sure,' agreed Jim. 'That's what it looked like at the time but we never thought then that maybe that's what we were supposed to think, that we were deliberately led west to take attention away from the more obvious route south from Rosewell.'

'Maybe you have a point,' Clem conceded.

'Reed and the others never figured we'd capture them but all the same they'd be laughing at drawing us away from the fourth man. Even then they'd be figuring on breaking gaol and linking up with Carlos again.'

'Why kill him? Why return when they would know they'd be shot down on sight.'

'Money, that's all it could be,' said Jim. 'Something went wrong and Carlos didn't have the money; they tried to get information from him and killed him. They've returned for the money all right and when they get it they're going to clear this country as if the hounds of hell were on their trail.' Jim eyed Clem squarely. 'And I've got to get 'em before they do or their trail will be colder than the winter snows.'

'Where do you figure on starting?' queried Clem.

'I reckon I've got to go back in time seeing you've no leads in the present,' said Jim.

'How do you mean?' queried Clem with a puzzled frown.

'I've got to suppose that my theory of a different route is right, that Carlsbad, Lakewood and Greenfield have some significance, maybe with the missing money.'

'You mean hiding-place?'

'Could be.'

'But the law never got near the fourth man, he'd have no cause to hide the cash.'

'The law didn't, but when it was known that we'd arrested three of the gang and were looking for a fourth who probably had the money then all the bent characters down here would be figuring on getting their hands on the loot. They had only one man to face and everyone would fancy his chances.'

Clem nodded slowly as he mulled over Jim's theories. 'Wal, I guess there could be something in what you say.'

'Yeah and it's the only starting point that I have.'

'Guess so. So you head down the Pecos tomorrow?'

'Now!' replied Jim starting to push himself out of the chair.

'You're not,' said Clem firmly. 'You've ridden far, slept rough I guess; you go now and you're going to be no good to face the like of Crazy Joe. You need a good night's sleep and some good wholesome food inside you. Besides what would Emma think if I let you go like that.'

Jim started to protest but when Clem cut him short he knew it was no use arguing and besides he knew Clem was right.

'Hi, Jim,' greeted Clem breezily as he entered the house by the back-door to find Jim enjoying a mug of coffee while Emma kept a watchful eye on the bacon sizzling in a pan. 'Sleep well?'

'Sure did,' smiled Jim, nodding his greeting. 'Mighty good to be in a bed again after the hard ground.'

'Good,' enthused Clem. 'Now you'll be fitter to face Crazy Joe and his sidekicks.' As he poured himself a coffee he glanced across at his wife. 'I fixed it up, Emma.'

Emma nodded. 'I'll pack two lots of food.' Her voice sounded a little heavy and, as she brought the pan to the table and started to fork out Jim's bacon, he glanced up and saw a concerned trouble in her eyes.

'You going somewhere, Clem?' Jim queried and he received the answer he half-expected.

'Yes, with you.'

'You ain't,' replied Jim firmly.

'Sure am,' grinned back Clem. 'Just fixed it up with the deputy.'

'But what about Emma?' put in Jim.

'It's my job, she knows that.'

Jim glanced at Emma who stood between the two men, the pan still in her hand.

'He's right, Jim,' she said, but the sadness and worry in her voice was not lost on Jim. He had heard the same tone in Kate's voice so many times when he had to go out on a job from which she could never be sure he would return. The fear that someone would out-gun him had been there and now he sensed it again in Emma.

'There's no need for you to wet-nurse me,' said Jim sharply as his gaze met Clem's.

'I ain't wet-nursing you,' returned Clem. 'But I ain't seeing you go against Crazy Joe and the others alone. Besides, it's my job to get after them – they're gaolbreakers, and the bank would still be mighty glad to get that money back.'

'He's right, Jim,' put in Emma without much enthusiasm. 'He's got to be on the look out for them. I've feared it ever since we heard they'd broken gaol. Wouldn't be natural if I didn't but there, I'm a sheriff's wife so I've got to expect these things and I've got to cope. Kate did. So it's better if you ride together.' She smiled wanly at Jim but behind it was the assurance of a woman who knew she was right and that no matter what he said Clem would ride with him. 'Now, get your bacon before it gets any colder.' She turned away to put the pan down as if to say there was nothing more to be said.

Jim eyed Clem. 'All right, I'm mighty glad to have you along. Didn't come here expecting you to ride with me, only came for information.'

'I know,' replied Clem. 'But you've given me more leads than I've given you. I had nothing to move on until you arrived and though they're only theories they've more possibilities than I had.'

'Another thing, Clem, and we're getting this straight from the start. You're the law with a right to take these men in but I want them first. No-one, not even you, is going to stop me taking them to Diaz once I catch up with them. So don't pull your tin-star on me.'

'I'll leave it behind if it'll make you feel any better,' said Clem as he started to unfasten his badge of authority. 'Might be better to do so,' he added as he put the badge on the table. 'Some hombres clam tight if they see a badge and we sure don't want that with such slender leads as ours. We need all the information we can get.'

Jim nodded but made no comment as he continued to enjoy his breakfast.

Half-an-hour later, their saddlebags packed, their slickers and bedrolls stowed, the two men bade Emma goodbye, heaved themselves into their saddles and rode out of Rosewell in the direction of the Pecos.

Reaching Greenfield they were pleased to ease themselves out of the saddles and seek a thirst-slaking drink in the saloon.

As they weaved their way between the tables to the long counter the bartender looked up from the glass he was polishing and his eyes widened with surprised recognition.

'Jim Hooper! Nice to see you. Didn't expect to see you in these parts again.' He glanced at Clem. 'Hi, Clem.'

Clem acknowledged him with a nod, as Jim spoke. 'Hello, Matt, you're looking good.'

'Can't grumble Mr Hooper.'

'Couple of beers, please, Matt, and one for yourself.'

'Thanks,' said Matt with a grin, 'but I still don't touch the stuff.' He started to draw the beer.

'So Eva's kept the reformed character she married,' said Jim. 'How is she?'

'Fine, thanks,' replied Matt, shoving the two foaming glasses across the counter.

'Is he looking after you?' asked Jim with a slight inclination of the head towards Clem.

'Sure,' answered Matt. 'No trouble around

here but no telling what might blow up after the gaolbreak.'

'You heard anything?' shot Clem sharply. The two lawmen were suddenly all attention with the hope that they might get a lead.

Matt looked from Clem to Jim. 'Say, is that why you're here, Mr Hooper?'

'Wal, sort of,' replied Jim.

'You be careful,' went on Matt, concern clouding his face. 'Crazy Joe threatened you at the trial and he ain't one to forget.'

Jim smiled. 'I'll be all right, Matt. Now, have you heard anything?'

Matt glanced at Clem. 'You keep your eye on him. Good men are hard to replace.' He leaned forward on the counter and lowered his voice as he spoke. 'I've heard nothing directly about the gaol-breakers, but you ain't the first to enquire.'

Matt and Clem exchanged looks and Clem, turning his eyes back to Matt, asked, 'Who else is interested?'

'Two hard cases. I figure they were in gaol same time as Crazy Joe and the others.

Heard them talking. I reckon they'd eaves-dropped on the three you'd put away.'

'And got a lead on the cash which was never recovered?' pressed Clem eagerly.

'Don't know about that,' returned Matt. 'I heard these hard cases mention Greenfield and Lakewood.'

'Could have heard that in gaol,' mused Clem. 'Could be your assumption is right,' he added turning to Jim.

'Anything else, Matt?' asked Jim.

'No,' replied Matt and moved to serve another customer further along the bar.

'I figure these two hard cases are a bit like us following a hunch,' commented Clem.

'Yeah,' agreed Jim, 'but I figure it helps to confirm we could be on the right trail.'

'So what do we do now?' asked Clem.

Jim looked thoughtful for a moment then said, 'If we're right that Carlos came this way and that he didn't have the money in Mexico and therefore hid it and that seems likely because Reed, Fallon and Parker wouldn't have come back otherwise. Maybe he split it in three.'

'Split the loot?' Clem looked puzzled.

'Yeah. That way if one lot was found they wouldn't be losing the entire haul.'

Clem nodded his agreement, and then suddenly catching up to Jim's idea, he said with some excitement, 'Three places have been mentioned, at least we assume so from what Chiquita said, so could the loot have been split three ways?'

'That's just what I was wondering,' agreed Jim. 'In which case Crazy Joe and his side-kicks have to come to Greenfield to collect.'

'So we wait,' suggested Clem.

'We'll give it a couple of days.'

Matt returned and pulled them two more beers.

'Where are these hard cases now?' asked Jim, after thanking him for the beer.

'That tall fella I just served, he's one of them.' Jim and Clem shot quick glances in the direction of the man leaning on the counter. He had a mean, rugged face which hadn't seen a razor for three days. His stetson, pushed back on his head, was battered and dirty, in keeping with his shirt and jeans. A gun was strapped low on his right thigh and Jim could just picture the long powerful fingers which cradled the glass of beer curling round the trigger while he enjoyed the satisfaction of a kill.

'The other?' Jim asked Matt.

'Left town yesterday.'

'Thanks, Matt. Oh, just one thing, can you remember a Mexican passing through here three years ago just after the bank robbery in Rosewell?'

Matt looked thoughtful for a moment then shook his head slowly. 'No, no. I think I would have remembered, we don't get many Mexicans through here.'

'Figured that would be your answer,' returned Jim. He turned to Clem. 'But that don't mean he didn't come this way; he'd more than likely keep out of sight.'

The two men finished their beers and left the saloon. After taking their horses to the livery-stable they looked in at the hotel on the opposite side of the street to the saloon.

Two days later they were sitting at a corner table in the saloon, reassessing the situation and considering whether they were wasting their time in Greenfield, when the batwings squeaked open. Automatically Jim and Clem glanced up from their beers.

'Fist Parker!' hissed Jim. Surprised excitement showed in his voice. He lowered his head and half-turned away from Parker's view. Clem slumped half-forward on the table so that he could keep the newcomer under observation. Their precautions paid off because, after a quick survey of the room in his first steps into the saloon, Fist continued on his way to the bar without another glance at the few people in the room.

Matt moved to serve him as he reached the counter.

'What's happening?' whispered Jim.

'Talking to Matt. He ain't ordering a drink. Matt's nodding in the direction of someone across the room near the foot of the stairs. Fist's leaving the bar. Crossing the room.

Talking to one of the girls. Now they're going up the stairs.'

Jim straightened and glanced in the direction of the stairs. The girl led the way with Fist only a step behind. They turned on to the balcony and, without a glance down into the saloon, entered the second room from the end.

As soon as the door closed, Matt came casually from behind his counter and, on the pretext of wiping tables down, came to that occupied by Jim and Clem.

'I figured you recognised him,' he said quietly as his cloth moved across the table.

'What did he want?' asked Jim urgently.

'Just asked me which was Fay,' replied Matt.

'Thanks,' said Jim and Matt moved away, gathered some empty glasses from another table and went back to the bar.

'Figure anything?' asked Clem.

'Puzzled,' replied Jim with a frown. 'He's by himself, so where's Reed and Fallon? He's a gaol-breaker, a wanted man, why risk being spotted just for a girl?'

'And I figure he has been spotted by that hard case,' observed Clem indicating the tall man who had been keeping his vigil from the bar each day. 'He's sure eyeing that room plenty, and he kept his face from Fist's view.'

Suddenly the second door from the end of the balcony opened and Fist Parker hurried to the stairs. He came down them quickly, a sense of urgency about his manner, and, without a glance around the room, bustled from the saloon.

The hard case pushed himself from the bar and followed without a moment's hesitation.

'Come on,' said Jim standing up. 'Can't let him take Fist.'

The two men started to move away from the table when a movement and a cry from the balcony stopped them in their tracks.

The saloon girl, her face streaming with blood, staggered out of the room and with a weak cry for help collapsed against the balcony rail.

Jim sized-up the situation in a flash and even as he rapped an order sharply at Clem, he was making for the stairs. 'Follow Fist!'

Clem needed no second instruction and was out of the saloon even as Jim reached the stairs. The saloon, which had been stunned into immobility by the sight of the battered Fay, suddenly erupted into an agitated uproar. Three girls and Matt ran to the stairs beating the other occupants of the saloon who surged after them.

'Keep 'em back, Matt!' called Jim over his shoulder.

The bartender swung round on the second step and faced the crowd. 'Hold it!' he yelled. 'Keep back!' He barred the way, exerting his authority so that the men hesitated, glanced up and settled into an anxious group buzzing with curiosity.

Jim dropped to one knee beside Fay who, in her semi-conscious state, was moaning with the pain. Blood flowed from an ugly cut on her right cheek and from another on the side of her forehead. Her eyes were closing as her face puffed beneath them. Her dress was torn and revealed sickening weals about her neck and shoulders, Jim winced; he knew she had felt Fist Parker's torturous fists.

'The doc! Water, towels!' Two of the girls moved instantly to obey Jim's authoritative words while the third cradled Fay's head gently as Jim lifted her in his arms.

They carried Fay into the room and laid her gently on the bed. The saloon girl comforted her with quiet words, reassuring her that she was in good hands.

The girl with the water and towels hurried into the room and started to clean Fay's face. Though she was gentle the pain seared through Fay and she winced and cried out.

The saloon girl whispered soothingly as she continued to administer her damp cloth. Suddenly Fay's eyes widened as much as they could as the pain seemed to force her out of her semi-conscious state.

'The bastard!' she hissed venomously.

'The bloody bastard!'

Jim, who had been standing anxiously by, was relieved by the outburst and stepped forward.

'Fay, Jim Hooper, ex-sheriff. I've got someone tailing your attacker and the doc's on his way. Why did he do it?'

Fay drew comfort from Jim's reassuring look. 'Didn't tell me his name,' she muttered between her swollen, split lips. 'Said a Mexican friend of his had told him to contact me about a visit I had from the Mexican three years ago.'

'Did he mention the Mexican's name?' asked Jim.

'No.'

'Do you know the Mexican's name from three years ago?'

'No.'

'Tell me what happened three years ago,' Jim urged.

Fay winced as her companion dabbed her forehead. She looked at Jim and seeing the need for information in Jim's eyes she went on. 'Nothing much to tell, really. I have a little house, well a couple of rooms really, on the edge of town. Most of the girls sleep here but I wanted a place of my own and Matt eventually let me.'

'Three years ago,' pressed Jim impatiently.

'Middle of the night I was awakened by a soft but urgent knocking on my window. When I looked out I saw this Mexican. He indicated he wanted to talk to me. He looked friendly enough but I was careful only to open the door a little. He asked me if he could rest up a while. He wanted nothing else and said he would be gone before daylight. He said he'd pay me well. He looked pretty well all-in and I agreed.' Fay licked at her swollen lips.

'Anything else?' asked Jim.

'I got him something to eat. He spent the rest of the night but was gone before sun-up.'

'He never said where he'd come from or where he was going to?'

'No.'

'He paid you?'

'I'll say. Best money I ever earned for doing nothing.'

'You told this to the man who came here tonight?'

'Yes,' Fay nodded weakly.

'This obviously didn't satisfy him – he beat you up.'

'Bastard,' hissed Fay venomously as Jim's words recalled the attack. 'He asked me where the money was. I didn't know what he was talking about. He didn't believe me. Said I was holding out on him. I couldn't tell him what I didn't know but it wasn't until after he'd done all this that he figured I must be telling the truth.'

'And were you?' asked Jim.

'Sure I was,' rapped Fay, her swollen eyes flaring defiantly.

'Anything else?'

'Wanted to know where I lived. Hit me again because I think the bastard enjoyed it and then left.'

'Thanks,' said Jim. 'Where do you live?'

Before Fay could answer the door opened and the doctor hurried in followed by the saloon girls.

As the doctor dropped on his knees beside the bed Fay glanced beyond him. 'Sal,' she said, 'show Jim where I live.'

'Thanks, Fay,' smiled Jim. 'You'll be all right with the doc.' He nodded to the medic who acknowledged it with a slight raising of his left hand. Jim looked at Sally. 'Come on let's go.'

They hurried from the room and went quickly down the stairs and, ignoring the querying glances, left the saloon.

'You figure this damned girl-beater is at Fay's?' asked Sally, as their feet clattered on the sidewalk.

'I sure hope so,' replied Jim. 'He wanted to know where she lived.'

'You know him?' queried Sally.

'Yeah. Fist Parker.'

'One of the gaolbreakers,' gasped Sally, the shock of the news causing her footsteps to falter momentarily. 'But what's he want with Fay? And why risk coming back to this area?'

'It's a long story, Sal,' replied Jim. 'When you can direct me to the house do so. It could be dangerous and I want you on your way back to the saloon as soon as possible.'

They had gone a few more yards when Sally slowed and then stopped just short of the corner of a side street.

'Turn right here, Jim, go to the next street running parallel to this one, not much of a street but turn left along it. You'll see two houses, shacks really, about fifty yards along. Fay's is the first one.'

'The other?' asked Jim.

'Mine.'

'Were you there three years ago?'

'No. I've only been there two years.'

'Anybody in it before you?'

'No.'

'Thanks, Sal,' smiled Jim. 'You get on back to the saloon.'

'And you go mighty careful,' said Sally with a serious concern.

Jim nodded and watched the girl hurry away before turning to the task ahead.

He hesitated at the corner, drew a deep breath and wiped the palms of his hands down the side of his trousers. He checked the hang of his holster and drew confidence from the feel of his gun-butt. His mind suddenly sharpened and he chastised himself for his feelings, but it had been three years since he had stepped out to face a man with a gun.

He moved cautiously round the corner and, keeping to the deeper shadows, worked swiftly but quietly along the street. Once he became active the feeling of apprehension which had gripped him momentarily had gone. Now he was the hunter closing in on his prey.

He was over half-way along the street when he instinctively felt another's presence. He stopped and tuned his senses to detect the other's position. Nothing. All was still. He waited. The darkness seemed to clamp around him defying his attempt at detection.

Still he waited. Still nothing. Maybe he had been mistaken. Maybe he was being extra sensitive after three years away from this sort of thing.

Jim was about to step forward when a slight movement about ten yards ahead of him caught his attention.

There it was again, hardly detectable, but definitely there.

Jim eased his Colt from its leather and with the utmost care moved forward stealthily. His eyes strained to pierce the gloom. There it was. A darker patch. A figure crouching low behind a barrel.

Jim tensed himself, then took one swift, silent step forward. 'Hold it!' he hissed.

The figure froze.

'Lay your gun down, careful like, and straighten,' whispered Jim.

The man did as he was told and as he stood up he turned towards Jim.

'Clem!' gasped Jim, relaxing as the man's identity became clear.

'Jim!' Clem was equally relieved. 'Thank

goodness it's you.' He bent down and recovered his gun. 'Hard case is at the corner, a bit cautious about following Parker.'

The two men crouched low.

'How's the girl?' whispered Clem.

'Beaten up but she'll be all right. Parker will be at her house looking for the money. Tell you later.' Jim's last words accompanied by a nod in the direction of the corner of the street and the partial outline of a man peering round it.

Suddenly the figure was gone. Instinctively, without a word Jim and Clem rose and hurried to the end of the street.

The moon filtered between the clouds revealing a man hastening towards the first of two shacks. As he disappeared round the far side of the shack, Jim and Clem ran forward swiftly but kept their footsteps as quiet as possible. Jim motioned for Clem to go to the left and the sheriff acknowledged with his hand.

Clem kept an eye on Jim's actions and when he saw him flatten himself on the ground beside the railings which surrounded the shack he did likewise. Both men crept forward until they could see the side of the shack which had been out of sight until now.

The hard case was peering through a window while from the inside came the sound of splintering wood. The man remained at the window until the noise stopped. Jim saw him move away from the window and turn towards the door, his gun held ready.

Jim's mind raced. He guessed from the ceasing of the noise inside the shack and from the fact that the man outside had turned towards the door, that Parker had found what he was looking for. Any moment he could step outside and Jim was certain that the hard case would fire first and ask questions later if Parker was alive. The hard case was going to take no chances, he wouldn't be bothered about exchanging words with Parker, all he would be interested in was the money. Eliminate Parker and take it. Jim wanted Parker alive!

He saw the man tense. It was slight but it

was there, the tension which comes to a man immediately before an anticipated action. Any moment Parker would appear.

Jim raised his Colt, took careful aim and squeezed the trigger gently. The shot crashed around the shack and in that same moment there was a maelstrom of movement.

The hard case jerked, staggered, spun and crashed to the ground. Fist Parker, who was half out of the door when Jim fired, leaped back into the house slamming the door behind him. In the same instance Clem sprang to his feet, jumped over the railings and raced towards the shack in a crouched run. Jim matched Clem's action, eager to reach the shack. They had their man cornered!

They were half-way to their objective when they heard a crash accompanied by the sound of breaking glass. A moment later they saw a figure racing away from the hut. Both men swerved to follow.

Jim's chest heaved with the effort. He loosed off a shot into the air as the figure, which could only be Fist Parker, reached the deep shadows of buildings closer to the main street. Jim and Clem drove themselves harder. They must not lose their man. Suddenly two shots sent them diving to the ground. Jim cursed as he held himself prone waiting for the next crash of a gun. But it did not come. Instead he heard the pound of running feet fading in the labyrinth of alleys.

Both men leaped to their feet and raced forward. Reaching the buildings they slowed, listening intently for any sound which would indicate the position of their quarry.

'His horse,' said Jim. 'It must be outside the saloon.'

Reaching the main street they saw the lights from the saloon reveal a small knot of people who had come on to the sidewalk at hearing the shots. They ran forward, all the time keeping a sharp look out for the slightest movement which might betray the presence of Fist Parker.

'Matt, anyone take a horse from the rail?'

asked Jim when they reached the group.

'No,' replied Matt, 'not since we heard the shots.' He looked sharply at Jim. 'Parker give you the slip?'

'Had to stop that hard case taking him. That gave Parker the chance to make a getaway. But he's still around. He'll need his horse.' Matt glanced round the group. 'All right, everyone inside and stay there.'

Matt shepherded the people back into the saloon and as he was about to push through the batwings himself Jim stopped him.

'How's Fay?' he asked.

'She'll be all right. Sore for a few days but nothing worse.'

'Good,' said Jim, relieved that there would be no permanent disfiguration. 'Get the doc to have a look at that hombre out at Fay's shack. Don't know whether he's dead or just wounded. Hadn't time to look.'

'Right,' said Matt and he left Jim and Clem on the sidewalk.

'Let's get out of sight,' said Jim. 'You take that corner and I'll take this one.'

Clem nodded and the two men separated to merge with the shadows in the alleys on either side of the saloon.

Jim grew impatient as the minutes ticked away. He had been so near getting the lead he wanted only to have it snatched from him by some no good hard case bent on trying to take a bit of easy money. Jim felt sure that the shadowy figure they had chased had been carrying something. Maybe Fist had found the money. He had certainly been tearing the shack apart. Maybe Carlos had hidden the money there. Maybe Crazy Joe and his sidekicks had persuaded him to talk before they killed him and the best way for him to identify the shack was to tell them to contact Fay. If these suppositions were correct why had Fist Parker come on his own why hadn't he had a back-up from the others in case things did go wrong? After all he had had to come openly into the saloon, a risk which had to be taken in order to identify and contact Fay. So where were Crazy Joe Reed and Blackie Fallon?

Jim had puzzled over this problem for close on twenty minutes when his thoughts were interrupted by the clatter of running feet on the sidewalk. There was an urgency about the pounding which occasionally faltered a little.

As the footsteps neared the saloon Jim stepped out of the alley.

'Pat, what the devil got you?' gasped Jim when the small, middle-aged, bearded man moved into the light from the saloon window.

The man who ran the livery-stable had an ugly gash across the side of his temple. The blood was congealing but it had streamed down the side of his face and had mingled with the dirt and dust to leave a mess which was in need of attention. His clothes were dishevelled and covered in dust.

'Some bastard jumped me. Slugged me before I had a chance,' gasped Pat.

'Did you get a sight of him?' queried Jim anxiously, as he was joined by Clem.

'No.'

Jim's lips tightened in a grim line. He was fearing he knew the answer and he felt it was confirmed when Pat added. 'Damned horse-thief.' Pat swayed and sought Clem's support.

Jim pushed the batwings of the saloon open and as Clem ushered Pat inside, Jim called out, 'Matt get the doc to see to Pat.'

The livery-man muttered his thanks and assured Clem he would be all right.

As the batwings squeaked shut behind him, Clem turned to Jim. 'Fist Parker?' Though he put it as a question he felt sure he was really making a statement.

'Guess so,' replied Jim, irritated that he had been outsmarted.

'Never heard a horse,' pointed out Clem.

'He'd lead it out of town so as not to draw our attention,' Jim pointed out.

'So, what now?' asked Clem, peeved that Parker had escaped when they were so close to taking him.

'Come on, let's get our horses,' said Jim and started in the direction of the livery-stable.

'We ain't got a chance of picking up his trail tonight and if we could he's got about twenty minutes' start on us.'

'Sure,' agreed Jim. 'Our lead has flown so all we can do is play a hunch. I had time to think about some things which puzzled me back there. Tell you as we ride.'

FIVE

Jim, with Clem alongside him, took the southern trail out of Greenfield and settled his horse into a steady, mile-consuming pace.

'Where we heading?' asked Clem.

'Lakewood.'

'One of the other two places you figure Chiquita heard mentioned,' observed Clem, still trying to puzzle Jim's reason for going there.

'Right.'

'But why? If we'd waited 'til daylight we might have picked up Parker's trail.'

'As I said, I'm playing a hunch hoping we can get a trick or two up on him,' replied Jim. 'Back there, waiting for Parker to show up, I got to thinking. We presume he found the cash at Fay's.'

'Sure. I figure he was carrying a sack or

small bag when he left there.'

'Right. And he was on his own.'

'Yes. If Crazy Joe or Blackie had been around we'd have known it.'

'Right again. Doesn't it strike you as peculiar that they weren't? That Fist was on his own?'

'Now you mention it, it does.' Clem puzzled. This was an aspect he had never thought of. 'But why on his own? It's unlike Crazy Joe to trust him with the money, supposing he found it.'

'That's what I figured so I puzzled over the fact that he was alone and tried to tie it in with any other fact that we knew.'

'And?' prompted Clem as Jim's voice trailed away thoughtfully.

'Well, we'd heard three places mentioned – Greenfield, Lakewood and Carlsbad.'

'Don't forget Rosewell,' Clem pointed out.

'Right. But that was where the robbery took place. Now suppose Carlos had split the money and had hidden it in three places.'

'Greenfield, Lakewood and Carlsbad.' An excited note had come to Clem's voice as he began to realise the line of Jim's reasoning.

'And there are three of them – Crazy Joe, Blackie and Fist.'

'You figure they split, each to recover the money from one of the places.'

'Seems more than likely; Fist was by himself in Greenfield,' said Jim. 'Lakewood is our next possible lead, though Crazy Joe or Blackie could have already collected the money hidden there. But it's a hunch we have to play and hope it gets us on their trail again.'

Clem agreed and settled himself more comfortably in the saddle to face a possible four hours ride.

Jim quickened the pace unaware that the pound of the hooves had reached the ears of a lone rider ahead and had caused him to leave the trail for the cover of some boulders.

Fist Parker slid from the saddle and moved to soothe the horse with whispered words while he held the animal steady. Tension gripped him as the sound of the horses on the trail grew louder and louder. He slid his Colt from its holster and held it ready for immediate action should it be necessary. He glanced skywards hoping that the clouds would keep away from the moon and enable him to identify the riders.

The hoofbeats grew louder. Then they were there, riders passing his cover.

Fist almost gasped with surprise when he recognised one of the riders as Jim Hooper and the other as the man who had ridden with him as deputy.

The two men rode on but it wasn't until the hoof-beats had faded in the distance that Fist allowed himself to relax.

'Jim Hooper, I thought you were long-gone out of this area,' he muttered as he swung into the saddle. 'It figures now who dropped that hombre outside the shack. How the hell did you get on to me? And now you're heading for Lakewood!'

He held his mount to the trail for half-a-mile then, thankful that he could remember side-trails and shortcuts from a life spent along the Pecos, he left it and sent his horse into an urgent pace along the quickest way to Lakewood.

He did not stop until he pulled his horse to a halt in front of the rundown hotel.

Entering the building he took the stairs two at a time to the first floor where he hurried to room seven, a prearranged meeting place for the gaolbreakers. It had seemed an ideal meeting place for them for the last inhabitant of Lakewood had pulled out a year ago, leaving it for the elements to take their toll.

The door squeaked protestingly as Fist flung it open at the same time shouting, 'It's Fist!' He didn't want anyone automatically grabbing a gun and shooting into the door-way.

Startled by his sudden entrance the two figures stretched on the floor sat upright but then, hearing Fist's voice, the alert tension drained from them and they cursed him loudly for their rough awakening.

'Glad you're here, Joe,' said Fist.

'We expected you'd be last to show up, you had the longest ride,' muttered Joe. 'Did you get the money?' he added with more enthusiasm.

'Sure did. Right here.' He swung the sack he carried to draw their attention to it.

'Great!' Joe and Blackie exchanged grins.

'Sure. And you?'

'Yeah, we got ours. Blackie had a hard time when he found the town deserted but he figured things out from what Carlos told us and so we've got the lot.'

'Good,' said Fist. 'Then let's ride. Jim Hooper and that there deputy he had are heading for Lakewood.'

'What!' Both Crazy Joe and Blackie gasped together.

'Don't pull no damned tricks here,' added Joe with an edge to his voice.

'I ain't kidding, Joe,' rapped Fist and the serious tone in his voice rammed his news home.

'Hell. I thought he'd left,' rasped Blackie.

'What's he doing back?' snarled Joe. 'And what the hell's he doing heading for Lakewood?'

Fist quickly told them of the happenings in Greenfield. 'Someone dropped that hombre waiting outside the shack,' Fist concluded, 'but it wasn't until I saw Hooper on the trail that I figured it must've been him who did it. But why he's heading for Lakewood...'

'After you,' snapped Joe irritably.

'Can't have picked up my trail,' rapped back Fist. 'Somehow he's done some guessing, so let's get to hell out of here.'

Crazy Joe had scrambled to his feet and now stood looking out of the window. 'Hold it,' he shot over his shoulder.

'What do you mean, hold it?' snapped Blackie. 'We've gotta ride.'

'We ain't riding,' came back Joe's remark coldly.

Blackie and Fist exchanged glances. Crazy Joe's nickname sure fitted him.

'But we've got the cash...' Fist's words

were interrupted by a cold, calculating voice.

'We ain't riding.' Joe turned slowly from the window and eyed his two sidekicks. 'Remember what Hooper did to us? Remember what I said I'd do? Well now's the chance.' Joe's eyes had narrowed as they filled with hate for the man who had sent them to gaol.

'Forget it,' pleaded Blackie. 'We can get away now.'

'And throw up the chance of blowing clever Mr Hooper's brains out.' There was a viciousness in Joe's voice and the two men recognised from the mad glint in his eyes that it was no good trying to protest or reason with him.

'We've got a God-made chance. The light's just coming up so Hooper will be an easy target as he rides in.'

'He's got someone with him,' Blackie reminded Joe.

'Fella that was his deputy,' said Fist. 'Clem Watson.'

'He ain't no hindrance. We'll blast him with Hooper.' Joe looked out of the window again. He observed the light streaking from the eastern horizon with some satisfaction. 'Fist, get your horse off the street and out of sight. Ours are in a stable at the back.'

Fist hurried from the room to carry out the order. He had seen Crazy Joe in this mood on several occasions, cold and calculating especially when he held the surprise hand. He would be all ready when Hooper and Watson rode in. The more Fist thought about it the more it seemed the right course to take. With Hooper eliminated their getaway would be easier.

Once he had taken his horse to the stable he gave it a quick rub-down, saw that it had some feed and then returned to room seven.

Crazy Joe had been putting some thought into their plan to greet Jim and Clem. 'There's a good position on the flat roof of that building opposite,' he said pointing it out from the window. 'Get yourself over there Fist. Blackie's going to be in the corner room at the end of the corridor. With its two windows he'll have a commanding view of the street and the approaches. Between the two of you you'll have Hooper and Watson in a crossfire.'

'And you?' queried Fist as he examined his rifle.

'I want to stare Hooper in the eye and see him grovel before he dies,' hissed Joe with venomous hate for the ex-lawman. 'I'll be on the street to meet him. You two be sure you have him in your sights when I call him out.'

'I'll take him,' said Fist. 'You'd better take Watson, Blackie.'

'Right,' agreed Blackie. 'But I still think we'd have been better riding out.'

'Like hell,' Crazy Joe swung on him sharply, anger flaring in his eyes. 'I want Hooper and this is the opportunity not to be missed. Now git, and Blackie,' he added, halting Blackie's instant move to obey. He eyed his sidekick coldly. 'Don't slip up!'

Blackie hurried from the room and clattered down the corridor. Fist left the room without a word and a few minutes later he was signalling he was in position on the roof.

Crazy Joe acknowledged the sign from the window of room seven. Satisfied, he checked his rifle and Colt and left the room for the street. He strolled to the end of the hotel where he saw that Blackie had placed himself beside the open window which gave him a view of the approaches to the ghost town. Joe raised his hand in an approving signal.

'I'll be under the awning across the street,' he called. 'Give me a signal from the other window when you see them coming.'

'Right,' called Blackie and settled himself to his vigil.

The first warmth from the sun was beginning to drive away the coolness of the early morning as Joe crossed the dusty street.

A forlorn chair still stood outside of what had been the store, its owner long-gone. Joe flopped into it after he had straightened and moved it into the doorway of the store. Hooper would sure get a surprise when he stepped out of the shadows. Joe grinned to himself, savouring the moment in his mind, as he settled down to wait.

'You tell me Lakewood is a ghost-town, died since I left?' said Jim, bringing Midnight to a halt.

'Yeah,' Clem confirmed.

'Then that means if part of the money was hidden in Lakewood there'd be no-one to contact about it as there was in Greenfield,' said Jim thoughtfully.

'Right,' agreed Clem.

'Then it might have taken longer in finding, if it has been found.'

'So you figure someone may still be around?'

'I'm being cautious,' grinned Jim. 'But better play it safe. Another thing, we must figure Fist was ahead of us and would tell the others of the trouble in Greenfield.'

'That might send them packing quick, if they figure someone's on their trail.'

'Sure, but they don't know it's the law; they

don't know it's us. If they haven't found the money I figure they won't run; they'll post a lookout while the search goes on.'

'Right. Then we shouldn't approach the town openly,' said Clem.

'Just what I was figuring,' agreed Jim. 'If I remember right, when we cross that next ridge we'll be in view from the town.'

'We sure will,' confirmed Clem. 'If we ride east aways we swing close to the town without being seen.'

The two men turned their horses eastwards and an hour later were prone on their stomachs observing the town from the cover of a small hill to the east of the silent buildings.

Jim exercised his patience watching for the slightest movement which would betray the presence of human beings. This was no time to slip up if Crazy Joe and his sidekicks were around and Jim had a feeling they were.

But there was no movement except for the tumbleweeds blown by the gentle breeze which had sprung up. It played with them, swirled the dust and forced unsecured doors and shutters to clatter and disturb the eerie silence which brooded in the deserted buildings.

'There's no-one there,' whispered Clem after half-an-hour. He automatically kept his voice low even though he knew no-one could overhear them. It just seemed the right thing to do in this place.

'Wouldn't be too sure,' replied Jim.

'But if Crazy Joe was here it would mean he hadn't found the money and if that was the case he'd be looking for it and we ain't seen any movement.'

'You're right,' agreed Jim. 'But I got this feeling. Let's play it cautious until we're certain.'

They lay there for another ten minutes before Jim suggested a move. 'We'll go in on foot,' he said. 'Leave the horses where they are.'

Clem nodded and followed Jim to his feet. They walked briskly towards the nearest building, their eyes and ears alert for anything which would indicate another presence.

Reaching the back of the building he opened its door gently. It squeaked in spite of his precaution but he hoped if there was anyone within earshot they would blame the wind.

The two men stepped inside the building and found they were in the livery-stable, the front doors of which were missing.

The wind moaned through the holes in the roof and puffed the dust across the opening which looked on to the main street.

The two men hurried quickly but silently forward stopping against the wall to one side of the opening. Jim inched himself so that he could peer into the street. A moment later, without looking round, he signalled Clem to come alongside him. As he did so Jim held out a cautionary hand. Clem moved with the utmost care.

'Across the street,' whispered Jim close to Clem's ear.

'Crazy Joe!' gasped Clem.

'Wonder if the other two are here?'

'We'd better suppose they are.'

'We'll watch for a while.'

Their precaution was rewarded after ten minutes during which time they saw Crazy Joe grow more fidgety. Suddenly he pushed himself to his feet and seemed to be annoyed about something as he stepped into the dusty street.

Reaching the middle of the roadway he stopped and stared northwards into the blue distance. After a few moments he moved forward a few paces and then looked up at the building on his left.

'Hi, Blackie,' his voice came clearly to Jim and Clem. 'Any signs?'

'No.' The voice was not as distinct to Jim and Clem.

'Blackie must be in a building,' whispered Clem.

Jim nodded. 'Corner room upstairs if he's to have a view of the north trail.'

Crazy Joe cursed at Blackie's information. 'Hell, are we going to have to wait all day?'

He swung round to face the building on the opposite side of the street. 'Hi, Fist, you damned sure it was Hooper and Watson you saw and that they were heading this way?'

Jim and Clem exchanged glances. So Fist Parker had spotted them. But where? Must have been after they had left Greenfield and when he identified them he must have ridden by another trail to Lakewood to warn Crazy Joe and Blackie. If so then why hadn't they run? Jim was puzzled until he remembered Crazy Joe's threat at the trial. And, even if he had got all the money, Crazy Joe was just crazy enough to jeopardise their chances of escape for the sake of revenge, especially as he would believe that he had the element of complete surprise.

'Yeah, sure I'm sure,' came the reply as Fist poked his head above the roof parapet. 'I'd know that bastard Hooper anywhere.'

'Well where the hell are they?' stormed Joe in frustration, kicking at a tumbleweed as it rolled past.

He spat into the dust, stared northwards

for a moment and then stomped back to his chair on the sidewalk, leaving only the wind to break the silence.

'We got 'em,' whispered Clem with some excitement. 'We know where they all are.'

'Right,' said Jim.

The two men moved away from the opening and then retreated further into the stable until they could keep Crazy Joe under observation from one of the stalls while they laid their plans.

Once they were satisfied, they hurried to the back door of the livery-stable where they parted. Clem headed for the building in which they figured Blackie was positioned while Jim headed in the opposite direction. Judging the distance, Jim turned into the third alley which would bring him to the main street. Stopping at the end of the alley he peered cautiously round the corner and was satisfied that he was now sufficiently far from Crazy Joe that at the right moment he would not attract Joe's attention when he crossed the street. Keeping Crazy Joe under observation, Jim waited for the next part of their plan to unfold.

As Jim was positioning himself, Clem was negotiating the first tricky part of their plan. Two blocks separated the livery-stable and the building he wanted to reach and between each block there was an alley leading to the main street. Clem needed to know where Joe's attention was, so at each alley he carefully surveyed Crazy Joe before he moved to cross the end of the alley. Each time he judged it nicely and crossed the intervening space without being detected.

Reaching the back of the hotel he gingerly pushed a door open and stepped inside. He moved slowly along the corridor leading to the lobby. A board beneath his feet squeaked. Clem froze, listening intently.

There was no sound except the moaning of the wind and the odd clatter as it shook a shutter. If Blackie had heard the squeak he must have put it down to the wind.

Clem moved on, tense to the situation, not wanting to betray his presence. He paused at the bottom of the stairs, glanced upwards and then started to climb with each foot carefully placed on the next step, feeling, probing so that he could transfer his weight without causing a noise. The minutes seemed years and Clem had to fight the desire to rush up and take Blackie. The noise would have upset their plans.

Reaching the landing, Clem paused and glanced along the corridor. Was this the floor on which Blackie was keeping his lookout or was he one floor higher? Clem glanced upwards and then back along the corridor. Would one floor higher be any advantage to Blackie? Clem searched his mind trying to recall his impressions of the hotel on the odd occasions he had been in Lakewood before it had become a ghost town. Before he could decide his mind was made up for him. Blackie cleared his throat.

Clem, every nerve in his body tuned for any eventuality, tip-toed quickly along the corridor. He reached the door at the far end and was thankful that it was slightly ajar. He peered through the gap and saw that Blackie was looking out of the window which faced the trail coming from the north.

He pushed the door gently but at the first sound of a squeak starting he moved swiftly and was into the room with his Colt close to Blackie almost before the gaolbreaker knew what was happening. Blackie's eyes widened in surprised amazement at the sight of one of the men he had expected to see riding along the trail into Lakewood.

'Not a sound!' hissed Clem.

Blackie glared venomously at Clem but could do nothing under the threat of the gun.

'All right,' said Clem, 'now do exactly as I say and don't try to pull anything.'

Blackie met Clem's piercing gaze and knew it would be useless to try to buck the lawman.

'Turn back to the window and call Crazy Joe over.'

'What'll I tell him?' asked Blackie, trying to play for a few moments in which he might find some way of outwitting Clem.

'You'll think of something,' rapped Clem. 'But make it sound good.'

Licking his lips nervously, Blackie turned slowly to the window and leaned on the sill. 'Hi, Joe,' he called loudly.

'Yeah, you seen 'em?' There was excitement and eager anticipation in Joe's voice. They heard a chair clatter on the sidewalk and knew Joe must be on his way.

Watching from the corner of the alley, Jim heard Blackie's call and tensed himself for Joe's reaction. He heard Joe answer and saw him push himself quickly to his feet, sending the chair clattering on the sidewalk. He crossed the street quickly towards the corner of the hotel, directing his gaze to the north trail hoping to see two dots betraying approaching riders.

That was the moment Jim had keyed himself for. As Joe's attention was drawn to the trail Jim launched himself from the alley and ran swiftly across the street. He gained the cover of the buildings on the opposite side and lost no time in making his way along the back of the buildings towards the flat-roofed erection on which he knew Fist to be. He figured Fist's attention might be drawn to Crazy Joe and he knew he would not have much time to act before Fist became suspicious by what he would see.

A barrel set at the corner of the building to catch rain-water gave Jim his chance. It was empty, dried by long days of sun. Jim turned it bottom-up and tested the wood. He climbed on to it and reached up towards the parapet. A slight jump and he was able to get a hold. He began to pull himself up slowly.

'What is it, Blackie?' called Joe as he crossed the street. His eyes searched the north trail hoping to see some indication that the man he wanted to kill was heading for his trap.

'Thought I saw something,' answered Blackie.

'Good,' whispered Clem and then with a short sharp effective blow brought the barrel of his gun across the back of Blackie's head.

As Blackie's knees buckled, Clem grabbed him and heaved him backwards away from the window. As the unconscious man slumped to the floor Clem stepped to take his place at the window. He was not a moment too soon for as he glanced down, Crazy Joe was moving into view.

'What was it you...' Joe's words trailed away into a pregnant disbelief. His eyes stared unbelievingly at the window and the gun pointing straight at him. And behind it was a man he had expected to be riding into Lakewood with Hooper. He froze in his tracks, his mind already trying to find some way out of his unexpected predicament. Maybe Fist would realise something was wrong when he heard no more conversation. But where was Hooper?

At that moment Jim was sliding over the parapet on to the flat roof. His eyes never left Fist Parker's back and as he climbed quietly to his feet he cradled his Peacemaker more comfortably in his hand.

When Blackie had called to Joe, Fist had alerted his attention to the north trail but could not detect any sign of movement. Wondering what Blackie had seen he glanced across at Joe who had stopped and was looking up at the window.

Nothing seemed to be happening. Joe's attitude seemed to be strange. These facts automatically registered in Fist's mind but it was only a moment later that they made their impact. Fist directed his attention more fully onto Joe. There certainly was something wrong. He pushed himself to his feet as the tension between Joe and Clem seemed to spark across to him, seemed to warn him of trouble. But what could it be? What could be wrong? Fist was puzzled.

'Hi, Joe, something wrong?' he shouted.

'No, everything's all right.' Fist was startled by the voice coming from behind him. It shouldn't be there and the fact that it was automatically brought him swinging round with his rifle held low against his hip. He knew instinctively that the owner of the voice had something to do with Joe's strange attitude and that whoever it was had to be eliminated. So at the moment of his turning his finger was squeezing the trigger.

But Jim, judging Fist's attitude correctly, anticipated his move and was already moving away from the spot at which he had spoken. Even as Fist fired Jim's finger pressured his trigger. The bullet took Fist in the upper arm causing him to lose his grip on his rifle as he tried to fire again. The weapon clattered to the wooden roof as, in spite of the pain, his eyes widened with disbelief at the sight of Jim facing him with a menacing Colt.

'You!' he gasped. 'How the hell did you get here?' He winced, tried to ease the pain with his hand. Blood trickled between his fingers and ran down his shirt sleeve.

'It's a long story,' said Jim as he stepped forward and relieved Fist of his Colt. 'Hold Crazy Joe there,' he yelled. 'We're coming over.'

His voice dashed Joe's hope that the

gunshots meant a way out of the dilemma. His brain raced. The money was in the room with Blackie, but his freedom meant more now. There must be a way. He didn't want to go back to that hellhole of a prison. Could he move fast enough to beat Clem's gun? He stared upwards. The gun was unwavering.

As if he had guessed the thoughts flying through Joe's mind Clem's voice came cold and menacing, 'Don't try it, Joe. I'll drop you before you move an inch.'

A few moments later Fist, still holding his arm, moved across the street in front of Jim. Crazy Joe said nothing as Jim, alert for any false move by either man, removed Joe's Colt. 'We're coming up, Clem,' he called, and indicated to the two gaol-breakers to head for the door of the hotel.

When they reached the first floor, Clem was standing in the corridor and his gun kept the two men covered as they moved sullenly into the room.

'Search 'em, Clem,' said Jim.

Clem holstered his Colt and, careful to keep the men between himself and Jim's Colt, he searched them for weapons. He took a knife from each of them and declared them clean.

'I need a doctor,' moaned Fist, feigning intense pain.

'Have a look at it, Clem,' Jim asked.

The lawman examined the wound quickly. 'A flesh wound. No permanent harm done. He'll survive the ride to Mexico. Bind it with your bandana, Joe.'

Joe did not move. He stared at the two lawmen. 'Mexico, you say? Ain't you turning us in?' He glanced at Clem. 'You ain't wearing a badge. What's going on?'

'Bind that arm Joe and then sit with your backs to the wall. Then we'll tell you exactly what's going on.'

As Joe was binding Fist's arm Blackie moaned and stirred. A few moments more even though his head still pounded from the blow, he was fully aware of their position and was sitting between Joe and Fist, listening to Jim.

'We ain't handing you over to the law yet,' explained Jim. 'We're taking you to Fernandez Diaz first.'

The name startled the three gaolbreakers and they stared up at Jim with amazement.

'What the hell for?' snapped Joe.

'So I can get my wife back,' replied Jim.

'You ain't making sense.'

'Diaz is holding my wife hostage. I have to deliver you three to him before he'll release her.'

'What the hell does Diaz want with us?' snarled Joe.

'You should know,' rapped Jim.

'Like hell we do.'

'You know him?'

'Only by reputation – a two-bit Mexican bandit,' replied Joe.

'Come off it,' said Jim with disbelief in his tone. 'You knew his brother. Wasn't he the fourth man in the bank raid? Wasn't he the one who got away with the money? When you broke out of gaol you crossed the border to contact him for your share of the loot only to find he hadn't got it, that for some reason he had hidden it as he rode south. You tortured him until he told you where then finished him off for trying to double-cross you.'

Joe and his sidekicks looked startled at Jim's words. 'Hi, hold on,' snapped Joe. 'We killed nobody.'

'We didn't!' shouted Blackie, backing up Crazy Joe.

'Carlos Diaz was murdered,' spat Jim. 'You three were seen.'

'Seen where?' snapped Fist.

'Crossing the border back into Texas.'

'That don't mean we killed Carlos.'

'Carlos's brother followed you but you beat him to the border. He daren't cross the Rio Grande and move deep into Texas so he called on me, took my wife hostage promising release when I took you three back to him alive.'

'You can't turn us over to him!' protested Blackie. 'Not for something we didn't do.'

'Don't protest your innocence,' rapped Jim. 'It won't do you any good. I'm taking you to Diaz.'

'Hold on,' stormed Crazy Joe. 'Let's get things straight.' Although hatred for the lawman burned in his eyes there was a serious light which caught Jim's attention.

'All right, let's hear your story,' pressed Jim.

'You're right about most things,' went on Joe. 'You've made some good guesses or played some hunches. Carlos Diaz was the fourth man and he did get away with the money. We led you on a false trail while he rode south.' Joe grinned at the memory of the way they fooled the law. Then his expression suddenly changed and malevolence returned as he went on. 'But you outsmarted us and that worried Carlos. He decided to hide the money and return to his brother in Mexico, and wait for our release.'

'Why didn't he take the money to Mexico?' asked Jim.

'We had no intention of going to Mexico

when we hit the bank but Carlos figured it the best thing to do after we got caught. He figured it would be a good place to lie low – with his brother – but he sure wasn't going to let him know about the cash, reckoned Fernandez would take the lot. At least Carlos had loyalty to us.'

Jim laughed harshly. 'And you murdered him for his trouble!'

'We didn't!' snapped Joe, his eyes smouldering angrily.

'How did you know Carlos was with his brother? You said none of you had any intention of going to Mexico,' put in Clem.

Crazy Joe looked at him contemptuously. 'Lawman, you know damned well there's ways and means of getting word into gaol.'

'So Carlos signed his own death warrant by letting you know where he had gone,' said Jim.

'Get it into your thick head, Hooper, we didn't kill him!' snarled Joe. 'We saw him, he told us where the money was, we were to get it and meet up with him in El Paso. Would we doublecross him after he had been straight with us?'

'Yeah, just what you coyotes would do,' said Jim, showing his contempt for the three men sitting on the floor. 'Now we've had enough talking, so on your feet and let's go.' He glanced at Clem, 'You take the cash and head on back to Rosewell. The bank will be mighty glad to see you.'

'I'm riding with you, Jim,' returned Clem. 'The bank have been without that cash for three years – they can wait a few more days.'

'I ain't running you into any more trouble,' Jim insisted.

'You've a long ride to take these three on your own,' said Clem.

Crazy Joe, who had scrambled to his feet, laughed mockingly. 'He's right Hooper. We'll take the first opportunity to split your skull wide open. And you gotta sleep some time.'

'I'm coming,' said Clem in a tone which indicated he would not consider Jim's proposal. Crazy Joe had made his point for him.

'Bring your wet-nurse along, Hooper,' grinned Joe, 'we'll have two heads to split instead of one.'

His two sidekicks standing beside him laughed with him hoping they would provoke the lawmen into taking some action in which they could gain the upper hand.

Clem started to rise to the bait but Jim stopped him. 'Leave it Clem,' he rapped sharply. 'Let's get going.'

Clem nodded and picked up the three sacks of money. Leaving the room first he preceded the bank robbers so that he could cover them from the front as they came down the stairs.

Dust swirled under the teasing fingers of wind as the five men stepped out on to the broken sidewalk.

'Where are your horses?' queried Jim.

'Stable back of the hotel,' answered Joe.

'Right, let's go.' Jim motioned with his gun.

The bank robbers led the way round the hotel and across the open space to the stable.

'Hold it!' rapped Jim when they reached the broken door. 'Against the wall.' The three men did as he ordered. 'Clem, dump the cash and go and get our horses.'

Clem dropped the sacks and started to move away.

'Hi, Watson,' called Joe, 'You leaving him on his own? Can't say we'll be here when you get back.'

Clem stopped in his tracks and swung round quickly. His eyes narrowed as he glared at Joe. 'Reed,' he hissed, 'if anything happens to Jim you'll always be looking over your shoulder wondering where I am. You'll not rest until I put you in your grave.' He shot a warning look at Fist and Blackie. 'And the same goes for you two.' He turned and hurried away.

Joe grinned and eyed Jim. 'Sure is some friend. Do you think you can hold us? Three to one.'

'But I've got the gun,' returned Jim.

'You wouldn't have time to take all three,' Joe pointed out with some satisfaction. 'One of us would get you.'

'Ah, you're right,' said Jim, a smile flicking the edges of his lips with some amusement. 'But which one will it be? Anyone like to make the first move?'

Wondering what he had in mind Blackie and Fist glanced anxiously at Crazy Joe.

'Looks like your two sidekicks are worried?' Jim pointed out casually. 'Neither of you two figure on making the first move do you?' He looked from one to the other. 'Seems you ain't got any support for that idea, Joe.' He paused then added, 'Sit down.'

As they waited for Clem to return, Joe searched for some way to outwit Jim but the ex-lawman had placed himself in such a position that only a gun would be effective and he held the weapon.

'Stow the money,' said Jim, once Clem was out of the saddle.

Clem soon had the money put away to his satisfaction.

'Right,' said Jim when he saw Clem make the final fastening on his saddlebags, 'you'll saddle your horses one at a time. You first Blackie.'

As Blackie scrambled to his feet, Jim indicated to Clem to follow him into the stable. A few minutes later Blackie emerged leading his horse, closely covered by Clem.

'You now, Fist.'

Fist took no longer than Blackie and finally Joe saddled his horse.

When Joe came out of the stable Jim noted the cold calculating look in his sunken eyes and he realised that up to now Joe's attitude had been one of bravado in the face of knowing that there was no chance of escape but from now on when things were going to be more difficult for the lawmen, Joe would be ever looking with cold calculation for a means of outwitting them.

It was going to be no easy ride.

SIX

Riding in single file on Jim's orders, the five horsemen inclined their heads to the sharpening wind as they left Lakewood to the wind, the dust and the tumbleweeds.

Clem led the way, with Blackie, Joe, Fist and Jim following. Even though he figured the gaolbreakers would not make a break without the money, Jim was ever-watchful for any suspicious movement. But none came and they progressed at a good pace throughout the day. By mid-afternoon both Jim and Clem felt sleep dragging at them for, apart from a brief stop on their way to Lakewood, they had had no sleep the previous night. The signs of their weariness were not lost on Joe and he noted them with deep satisfaction. Maybe tonight he'd be able to make the break he wanted.

It was early evening when Jim called the final halt of the day on an open patch of ground close to a stream in the lower reaches of the Sacramento Mountains.

'Feeling weary, Hooper?' Joe accompanied his mocking words with a harsh laugh.

Jim ignored the question and drew his Colt. 'Fix your horses over there,' he ordered, nodding in the direction of the stream. 'You too, Clem.'

In a few minutes four horses had been watered and unsaddled and finally tethered securely for the night-stop.

With saddles laid out around a point chosen for a fire Jim ordered the three bank-robbers to sit down. 'Tie 'em up,' he said to Clem.

Careful not to put himself between the men and Jim's gun, Clem completed his task efficiently. With their feet tied at the ankles and their hands secured behind their backs, Jim figured he could relax. They couldn't give him any trouble. He slipped his Colt back into its holster and slid from the saddle.

While Jim attended to his horse Clem got a fire going and before long some coffee and food were ready.

Jim and Clem filled their mugs with steaming coffee and piled their plates with stew made with the meat Emma had supplied.

'Hi, how about us?' called Joe as Jim and Clem sat down on the opposite side of the fire to the three bankrobbers.

'All in good time,' replied Jim. 'You ain't in a privileged position right now.'

'We're as hungry as you are,' protested Blackie.

'There's plenty,' rapped Clem. 'You'll get some. Now just shut your traps and don't spoil this for us.'

'Mighty big when we have our hands tied, aren't you?' sneered Joe.

Clem stopped eating, looked up and met Joe's contemptuous eyes.

Jim glanced at Clem. He felt the tension mounting in the man beside him. He saw his jaw tighten and his nose twitch. He recognised the signs he had come to know when Clem was his deputy.

'Cool it, Clem,' he whispered sharply. 'Don't let them needle you.'

Clem stared hard at Joe for a moment longer then let the tension run out of him and he returned his attention to his meal.

Though Joe and his sidekicks tried to provoke their captors Jim and Clem continued to take no notice. When Jim saw that Clem had finished he drained the last drops of coffee from his mug and looked across the dancing flames to the three men.

'If you're finished yabbering you can have something to eat,' he said tersely.

'We can't eat trussed up like this,' moaned Blackie.

'Sure you can't,' agreed Jim as he got to his feet, 'so we're going to untie your hands. Just one thing – don't try to be smart; there's a Colt here that won't mind dropping you and the rest of the journey won't be pleasant with a shattered leg.' His voice was cold, threatening, leaving the men in no doubt as to what would happen if they tried to outsmart the lawmen. Jim glanced at Clem who was standing beside him. 'All right, untie their hands.'

A few minutes later their hands free from the bonds the three men were wolfing into the food while Jim kept a watchful eye for any false move.

As vigilant as he was he was not near enough to hear Fist's whisper between mouthfuls. 'Joe, distract his attention when he ties us up.'

With a slight inclination of his fork Joe acknowledged.

When they had finished Clem went to refix the ropes.

'Say, ain't you scared with all that money in your saddlebags?' asked Joe, glancing over his shoulder at Clem who had moved behind Fist.

Clem looked at Joe as he wound the rope round Fist's wrists. 'Why should I be? You three ain't going to get near it.'

'Don't be too sure,' grinned Joe. 'I

wouldn't sleep easy if I were you.'

'I'll sleep all right. I'll have no worries about you.' He gave the rope a final knot and moved behind Joe, failing to notice that Fist had had his huge hands tightly clenched.

A few moments later he rejoined Jim, who relaxed.

'Guess they'll trouble no-one,' said Clem. 'Are we setting a watch? I'll take first turn if you like.'

'Don't think it's necessary,' replied Jim. 'I guess you feel just as whacked as I do. We need all the sleep we can manage and we want an early start.'

'How long you figuring on taking?' asked Clem as he threw some more wood on the fire sending sparks streaking upwards.

'We've a hard ride tomorrow to get over Guadalupe Pass but I reckon we should make Salt Flat before nightfall.'

'Then El Paso?'

'No. I'm going to push hard across country, cross the Rio Grande near Acala and hope to make Diaz's hangout before night.'

141

'That'll be a long ride,' said Clem doubtfully. 'Might be better to spend an extra night.'

'Might have to,' agreed Jim as he adjusted his bedroll. 'But I want Kate out just as soon as I can.'

'Sure,' agreed Clem.

'So we need all the sleep we can get.' He glanced across at Joe and his sidekicks who were trying to shuffle themselves into more comfortable positions. 'Guess we'd better throw a blanket over each of them.'

'Or let 'em cool off,' said Clem.

He followed Jim over to the three men who nodded their appreciation as the blankets fell over them. 'Get some sleep, you've a long, hard ride tomorrow.'

'Hi, you serious about taking us to Diaz?' said Joe, 'or are you dumping us on some remote mountainside and taking off with the money? I'm beginning to wonder if Diaz really has your wife.'

Jim stared hard at Joe. The flickering flames lit up the grimness of his expression. 'You're going to Diaz, make no mistake about that.'

'But you can't hand us over to him, it ain't right,' protested Joe. For the first time there was a touch of alarm in Joe's voice. 'You're the law, you gotta take us in, you can't hand us over to a damned Mexican.'

'I can and I will,' rapped Jim and the tone in his voice left Joe in no doubt as to what their fate was.

'Hell, we're Americans same as you; you can't hand one of your own kind over to a bastard like Diaz.'

'You ain't the same as us,' hissed Jim. 'You're on the wrong side of the law and…'

'Maybe,' snapped Joe, 'but that don't give you the right to do as you please with us.'

'I want my wife back safe,' rapped Jim with a harshness to his voice. 'And you are necessary for that, so you go to Diaz.'

'You're trading lives. You know what Diaz will do!'

'Sure. But it's only what you deserve after what you did to his brother.'

'We did nothing to him!' protested Joe.

Blackie and Fist who, until now, had only listened to the exchanges lent support to Joe's statement.

Jim's eyes narrowed as he glared at the three men. 'You killed him to find out where the money was.'

'We didn't!' all three protested vigorously.

'Then why didn't Carlos ride with you?' demanded Jim.

'He didn't want to raise his brother's suspicions. He was not like his brother and had only used him as a safe place to hide until we contacted him again. Like I told you we were going to meet him in El Paso after we had picked up the money.'

'A likely story coming from the likes of you. You wouldn't consider your grandmother let alone Carlos,' spat Jim with contempt.

'We didn't kill him,' hissed Joe viciously. 'Hi Watson, you're the law, not this bastard; you can't let him overrule you.'

Clem did not reply and Jim turned from the three men.

Both men removed their gunbelts and

when they laid down they placed their Colts, free from their holsters close at hand.

'Jim,' called Clem quietly, 'could they be telling the truth about not killing Carlos?'

'Who else would want him dead?' countered Jim.

'Don't know,' returned Clem, 'but they declared innocence fairly strongly.'

'Sure, that's only natural. I figure they're guilty.'

'What about this point that Carlos and his brother didn't get on together?'

'Be careful, Clem. Joe didn't say they didn't get on, he only said they were different.'

'But he implied it.'

'That's your interpretation, someone else would think differently.'

'You knew the Diaz brothers, what do you think?'

'Well,' replied Jim thoughtfully, 'I know little about Carlos, only met him a couple of times. I agree he's different from Fernandez but I have no reason to suppose they didn't see eye to eye. No, Clem, I think they tortured Carlos to find out where the money was and then killed him so that he could put no-one on their track. Unfortunately for them Fernandez wanted revenge, something they hadn't reckoned on, and I, who had arrested them after the bank robbery, happened to be the man Fernandez could use. In any case, whether they're guilty of Carlos's death or not, they go to Fernandez. I want Kate back!'

Clem knew there was no more to be said and, with a final glance across the fire at the prisoners, he settled down for the night.

Sleep came swiftly to the two lawmen after so little rest since leaving Greenfield.

After an hour the flames had lowered but the glowing fire still cast a circle of light over the forms round it.

Fist raised his head slowly and glanced across the light. The two lawmen were still and breathing heavily. He tested the bonds around his wrists hoping that by clenching his fists while being tied he had gained sufficient slack, when he relaxed his hands, to play on.

Fist tested his bonds again. They were slacker than they were the first time he had been tied. Maybe he could do something. He began working his wrists, straining at the rope. Ten minutes later, with sweat pouring from him, in spite of the sharpness of the night air, he seemed no nearer breaking loose. Though the bonds were slacker he could not wriggle his wrists free nor reach the knots with his fingers. He needed help, someone to work on the knots.

He raised his head slowly and glanced once more at the two sleeping forms across the fire. They had not moved and still they were breathing heavily. Fist carefully turned the blanket off himself, and rolled over towards Joe.

'Joe,' he whispered.

The form beside him stirred.

He repeated the word and this time Joe came wide-awake. He turned to Fist.

'Joe, I worked it so my ropes were slacker. Back to back you may be able to work on

147

the knots.'

Joe nodded, realising that the less they spoke the better. He glanced at the two lawmen. They were sound asleep.

Joe and Fist wriggled until they were back to back and Joe was able to touch the knots on Fist's bonds. His fingers worked swiftly but after a quarter-of-an-hour anger was mounting in him when he felt no progress in his efforts. Suddenly the anger vanished as a wave of excitement swept over him with the easing of one section of rope.

His fingers worked faster, pulling, pushing, easing, straining. If only he could do it then he'd give the clever Hooper the shock of his life. The thought of what he would do, of how he would enjoy tormenting the ex-lawman before finally killing him spurred him on to make a greater effort.

The rope gave a little more, and then some more. Fist felt the slackness increase and worked his hands to help. Suddenly the rope gave completely and his hands were free. He curbed the urge to yell with triumph and instead sat up slowly. Whatever happened they must not spoil things by over-enthusiasm. The sleeping forms had not moved. He untied the ropes binding his legs and rubbed them sharply to restore the circulation.

Crazy Joe waited patiently. As eager as he was to be free he dare not urge Fist to be quick. Then Fist was kneeling beside him working swiftly on the ropes which tied his hands. As soon as they were free Fist started to move to Blackie but Joe stopped him with a restraining hand and shake of the head. Fist did not question for it had always been a rule among them that when they were together Joe was the leader.

Joe unfastened his ankles and rubbed them while Fist kept his eye on the sleeping lawmen. As they crouched together, Joe pointed to Fist and then towards Clem. Fist nodded his understanding. They rose quietly and, half-crouching, half-running, they moved silently in quick short paces towards the sleeping forms.

Joe's mind pounded more and more the

nearer he got to Jim as the excitement of anticipated revenge heightened.

He paused a moment over the still form of the ex-sheriff, over the man who had sent him to gaol. The intense desire for revenge burned deep. Joe started to bend down and reach out for the gun. Suddenly, with the swiftness of a rattlesnake, Jim's hand closed around his gun and started to swing it towards Joe. Startled as he was by the swiftness and surprise of Jim's action, Joe, driven hard by the nearness of freedom and revenge, dropped suddenly, his clawlike fingers closing round Jim's hand, forcing the gun away from himself.

Jim heaved under the blanket tossing Joe to one side but Joe clung to the wrist taking Jim over with him. In spite of the tangle of blanket Jim drove his right knee upwards into the pit of Joe's stomach. Joe grunted as the pain seared through him and the breath hissed out of him. His grip on Jim's wrist weakened and Jim tore himself free. He pushed himself backwards on to his heels and straightened with his Colt pointing at Joe.

'Hold it!' he rapped loudly, 'or Joe gets it!'

The harsh command in his voice brought the struggle between Clem and Fist to a sudden end.

'You all right?' Jim called to Clem as the two men scrambled to their feet.

'Yes,' replied Clem. 'Thanks for the warning.'

'Warning?' gasped Fist, staring disbelievingly at Clem.

'Sure,' grinned Jim, amused by the dark annoyance which crossed Joe's face in spite of the pain. 'We've been waiting five minutes for you to make your move!'

Fury burned in Joe's eyes as he scrambled to his feet still holding his stomach.

'What the hell's going on?' yelled Blackie.

'Joe and Fist tried to get smart,' answered Clem as he motioned Fist back to his side of the fire.

'Why the hell didn't you free me?' stormed Blackie as Joe and Fist came back to their bedrolls.

'Guess Joe had his mind too much on revenge, wanted to get on with it as soon as he was free,' answered Fist.

'Look where it got you!' snapped Blackie. 'If you'd freed me first we'd have out-numbered them.' Anger toned his voice as he went on. 'If you'd have listened to me in the first place we'd never have been here; we'd have cleared from Lakewood with the money long before Hooper arrived.' His eyes blazed at Joe. 'You and your revenge!'

'Shut up,' hissed Joe, angry with the humiliation of being outwitted once more by Jim. His eyes narrowed as he faced Jim. Reflections from the fire heightened the hate in them. 'Don't think we're finished yet, Hooper. We've got a long way to go.'

Jim did not answer. A few moments later the two gaolbreakers were tied up once more.

'Sorry about that!' Clem mumbled his apologies as he and Jim returned to their blankets. 'Guess I must have left the rope a bit slack.'

'Forget it, Clem. No harm done,' Jim reassured him.

'There might have been.'

'Well there wasn't so forget it. But it's a warning, we'll have to look out for ourselves.'

It was a hard ride the next day, ever-climbing towards Guadalupe Pass dominated by the snow-capped Guadalupe Peak towering another three thousand feet above the pass.

Jim brought up the rear of the small cavalcade. He was ever-watchful for any attempt at escape. Though there were times when he figured any of them might try he figured he held two deterrents – his Colt and the money. He could not visualise Crazy Joe making an attempt without the money; they had risked a lot to get it and with it still in Clem's saddlebags there was still the temptation to try to get it back.

They crossed the pass and beyond lay the descent to the Salt Basin and on to the salt flats on the edge of which Jim figured they would make their second night's camp.

They had been coming down slowly for about an hour when the track swung round a sharply rising rock-face with a drop on the left-hand side and narrowed to a width sufficient for only two horses.

Suddenly Joe kicked his horse sharply, sending the animal leaping forward through the narrow space between Blackie's mount and the rock-face. He was on to Clem before the lawman realised anything was happening. A pounding blow in his back sent Clem flying from the saddle and in the same movement while keeping his horse to a fast run Joe swept up the reins of Clem's horse. Frightened by the sudden commotion the animal was only too glad to be taken away from it and it surged after Joe.

Clem hit the rock trail hard, driving the breath from his body as he slid towards the edge of the drop. As the danger impressed itself on his mind it drove out the surprising suddenness of the initial action. He twisted and dug his feet against the surface rock, trying desperately to find some purchase to slow him down. He found it and in the last few feet jerked to a stop.

It was all over in a matter of moments, almost before Blackie and Fist could realise what was happening. Trying to seize the opportunity of the confusion caused by Joe's break they started to urge their horses forward only to check them suddenly as a shot from Clem's Colt whined over their heads.

'Hold it!' he yelled and the two men saw themselves staring at the muzzle of the gun held by a prone Clem. They steadied their mounts which, frightened by the noise, tugged to get away from it.

Jim was taken completely by surprise at the unexpected suddenness of the action but even as Clem hit the rock he was urging his horse past Fist. The noise of Clem's shot crashed around his ears as he sent his horse past Blackie. The animals collided but their riders held them to their bidding, Jim forcing Midnight forward on the trail.

As he rounded the bend Jim saw that Joe was already some considerable distance down the slope. He urged his horse faster and, though the animal did not like the surface beneath its hooves, it answered Jim's call.

By the time the trail had moved away from the sheerness of that part of the mountain and away from the rocky surface Jim had gained a few yards. Now he called for greater speed and Midnight stretched himself across the softer ground. Cutting hooves pounded the turf and Jim knew that for Joe hampered as he was by a second horse, there was no escape.

Almost at the same time a desperate look over his shoulder conveyed the same impression to Joe, but he had snatched the money and no way was he going to just let it go. Fury bit deep at him. Was he going to be outsmarted again? If only he had a gun!

The pounding of the pursuing horse grew louder and louder thundering its message of capture into his mind.

He glanced over his shoulder. Jim was alongside Clem's horse. Joe snatched at a chance. Suddenly he released the grip on the reins which were leading Clem's mount. The animal swerved crashing against Midnight who shied away from the other animal. At that moment Joe was hauling hard on the reins bringing his animal to an earth-tearing halt. At the same time he turned it sharply. For one moment it seemed as if the horse would fall but Crazy Joe handled it skilfully and had it under control in a charge towards Jim.

Realising that he had lost ground Jim was trying hard to get Midnight under control on a track which would take him after Reed again. He succeeded and looked up to measure the distance he had lost only to find Crazy Joe Reed bearing down on him fast.

Jim had no time to get out of the way. He was almost frozen by the surprise of the unexpected sight of Joe looming at him.

Joe measured his distance and launched himself from the saddle. His right shoulder took Jim high on the chest and his arms encircled him, carrying him out of his saddle.

As soon as he felt the release Joe let his grip go and both men crashed to the ground independently. Joe had already formulated his action and as he hit the ground he knew what he was going to do. Jim, on the other hand, hit the ground still in a state of surprise but immediately he crashed to the earth his mind functioned crystal clear. He was aware of Joe launching himself at him, arms outstretched, hands reaching for his throat. Jim twisted to one side and felt the fingers graze down the left-hand side of his neck but he was half-pinned to the ground by Joe's body.

He brought his right arm over. His hand closed on Joe's shoulder. In the same movement he pushed hard and heaved with his body to get extra momentum. He hurled Joe off him and then rolled after him. As their bodies clashed Jim drove his fist hard at Joe's head. Joe turned his head and the blow glanced off his temple. Joe pulled his knees up giving himself leverage to push Jim away. At the same time his clawlike fingers groped for Jim's Colt. Jim felt the movement and, even as he was propelled off Joe, his fingers closed vice-like round Joe's wrist. As he rolled he dragged Joe with him and at the same time drove his other fist hard to Joe's face.

The opposite momentums met with a sickening thud and Jim felt Joe go limp. Gasping for breath he shoved the inert body away and scrambled to his feet. He stood panting and looking down at the unconscious Joe Reed until he got his breath back.

Jim wiped his hand across his forehead and ran fingers through hair. He looked round and saw that the horses had not gone far and were now standing nuzzling at the ground. A glance told him that Crazy Joe would not come round for a few minutes so, retrieving his stetson, he slapped the dust from his clothes and hurried to collect the horses.

As he neared the figure on the ground on his return Joe stirred and moaned. His eyes flickered open and closed immediately against the bright light. Joe shook his head trying to drive away the muzziness. His eyes flickered open several times as he got used to the sunlight. Finally they stayed open and focused sharply on Jim, who was standing over him.

Joe's lips set in a grim line. 'Damn you, Hooper,' he hissed. 'Damn you to hell.'

'You looking to be gunned down,' snapped Jim. 'If I hadn't wanted you alive you'd have had a bullet in you by now.'

Joe only glared back at the man whom once again he had failed to outwit.

As Joe started to struggle to his feet Jim pushed him back to the ground with his foot. 'Stay right there,' he ordered. 'There ain't a better place for you until the others get here.'

'You figure Watson'll get here?' There was a note of derision in Joe's voice as he recalled the way he had dealt with Clem.

A confident smile flicked Jim's lips in reply. 'When I lit out after you Clem had his gun on your sidekicks.'

Joe's face clouded with anger. 'Hell, what're those two bastards doing? I gave them a chance. They're as slow as old squaws.'

Joe lapsed into a morose silence and Jim, while keeping Joe under surveillance, watched the trail.

It was not long before two men appeared on foot while a third rode behind them leading a second horse.

'Good idea to give them some exercise,' grinned Jim, amused at the discomfort of Blackie and Fist.

'Thought it might take some of the spunk out of them,' laughed Clem as he swung out of the saddle. 'You all right?' he asked with concern as he turned to face Jim.

'Sure,' replied Jim. 'Everything worked out.' He turned to the gaolbreakers. 'Mount up,' he ordered curtly.

'Hell, give us a break,' moaned Blackie from the ground where he and Fist had sunk beside Joe.

'We ride NOW!' snapped Jim, motioning with his gun for them to move. 'And don't try any more tricks,' he added as they scrambled to their feet.

The ride to the salt flats went by without any more incidents, and that night Jim and Clem took it in turns to stand guard.

The following day Jim pressed hard for the river but Joe deliberately caused some minor delays to slow the pace. There was little Jim could do to counteract a horse supposedly going lame, a bedroll which fell off a horse and had to be recovered or a man who slipped when mounting his horse and feigned a damaged ankle.

By mid-afternoon Jim was resigned to having to spend another night on the trail and he had to curb his eagerness to reach Kate as soon as possible. He had to agree with Clem when the lawman pointed out that it was better to arrive at Diaz's place in daylight.

Joe sensed the annoyance in Jim at having to lay-up for one more night. 'You ain't made it yet, Hooper,' he mocked as they made camp.

Jim spun round sharply on Crazy Joe. 'I'll get you there,' he snapped. 'And don't any of you try anything. I might not be so easy on you next time!'

'Don't forget Diaz wants us alive,' countered Joe.

'Alive, sure. Dead you aren't any good to me – but maimed, you are.'

Only the night sounds and the crackle of the fire broke the silence which had settled on the Texas countryside.

Jim took first watch and pulled his coat more tightly around him to combat the chill night-air.

'Hi, Hooper,' called Joe, 'what's it going to feel like when you find out you've handed three innocent men over to Diaz?'

Jim chose to ignore the question and held his hands out to the warmth of the fire.

'We didn't kill Carlos.' Joe's statement brought murmurs of support from his two sidekicks. 'Do you think we'd kill the man who had played right by us?'

''Course we wouldn't,' put in Blackie

when Jim did not reply. 'He could have rode off with the money, but he didn't.'

'Good man, Carlos,' added Fist rising to the idea that Joe wanted to keep the pressure on Jim. 'Deserved better than being murdered.'

'Still been alive if he'd ridden out with us as we wanted him to,' pointed out Blackie.

'Sure would,' agreed Joe. 'I'd like to get my hands on the bastard who did it. Hooper, handing us over to Diaz ain't going to find the killer. Besides, what are the authorities this side of the border going to say when they learn you didn't take us in but handed us over to a damned Mexican and a no-good one at that?'

'Wouldn't like to be in your boots,' said Fist.

'Nor would I,' said Blackie.

'And what about Watson? He's still wearing a badge. What'll it be like for him? Ever thought of him, Hooper? Ever thought of what it'll do to him as a lawman?'

Jim stirred. He had tried to ignore their

words but could not shut them out. They were right, he had gone against the right way of doing things. They should have been handed over to the law in Texas. But there was Kate and that pressure on him had been too great. He could not ignore his wife for the likes of Crazy Joe and his sidekicks. But he had implicated Clem and he had no right to do that.

'Clem had his chance to opt out when we got you three and the money. In any case who'll be worried what happened to you three when the money is handed over?' Jim spoke more to convince himself than to answer Joe.

'You still intend to leave us with Diaz?'

'I want my wife back unharmed.'

'But you can't just give us to Diaz,' protested Fist. 'Not when we didn't murder Carlos. Hell, you know what'll happen to us.'

'I have an idea. But do I care?'

'You can't do it!' The alarm creeping into Joe's voice spilled over onto his two companions.

'Give us a break, Hooper,' gasped Blackie nervously as the thought of what Diaz might do to them came home.

'Yeah,' said Joe. 'Give us a chance. We'll split some of the money with you.'

'Sure will,' said Fist seizing eagerly onto Joe's suggestion.

'And we'll help you get your wife back!'

'Stow it,' rapped Jim. 'I wouldn't trust you coyotes as far as I could throw you.'

'Sure you can. Carlos did,' spat Joe, emphasising the last two words to support his claim that they were innocent of his murder.

'And look where it got him,' replied Jim sharply.

'I tell you we didn't kill him!' Joe's voice rose angrily. 'Hell, what's it take to drum it into your thick skull!'

'I'm taking you to Diaz!' Jim's voice was cold with determination. 'Now shut up and get some sleep.' Jim pushed himself to his feet and strolled away, putting an end to the matter.

The following morning Jim had everyone

up early. The sun only just breaking the eastern horizon when the five men mounted their horses. He was anxious to be on his way, anxious to get this job over. He knew it was going to be a tricky day and he sharpened his watchfulness and advised Clem to do likewise.

They made good time to the river and Clem was making straight for the ford when Joe checked his horse. His action was followed by Fist and Blackie.

'Hold it, Clem,' called Jim as he stopped Midnight to hold his position behind the three gaolbreakers.

Clem stopped and turned his horse. He slid his rifle out of its scabbard and sat facing the other riders.

Joe glanced sharply at Clem and then turned in his saddle to see Jim's Colt facing him. There was no way they could make a run for it.

'Well, Joe, what is it this time?' asked Jim calmly, his eyes never leaving Joe.

'Once we cross that river we're into Mexico

and I don't fancy our chances with Diaz. Give us as chance, Hooper.' The pleading tone had come to Joe. This was something Jim had never experienced nor expected from Crazy Joe Reed.

Fist and Blackie murmured their agreement.

'Apart from getting my wife back safely I don't care what happens to you,' replied Jim.

'Come on, Hooper, you can't...'

Joe's plea was interrupted by Jim. 'If you didn't kill him who did? You've never even offered a suggestion of another killer. You had a good motive – more money for yourselves. You told me that no-one else knew about the money, so no-one else could want to kill him for information. Besides, if there was another killer wouldn't he have been looking for the money?'

'He'd have had to be a Mexican,' put in Clem. 'Diaz never mentioned any other white man around his encampment, only you three. That right, Jim?'

'Sure is,' agreed Jim. 'You told me Carlos did not get on with his brother. I agree they were different but I never saw any antagonism. In fact as far as I could see Carlos kept very much to himself.'

'Diaz could have killed him,' suggested Joe eagerly.

'You've no reason to suggest that,' replied Jim tersely. He was getting fed-up with the delay. 'If Diaz had killed him there'd have been a Mexican looking for that money and we never saw one. Besides, if Carlos didn't take the money back to Diaz's encampment it's hardly likely he would tell him about it and if Diaz didn't know about the money he had no reason to kill him. Now, quit stalling and ride.' Jim moved menacingly towards the three men.

Clem raised his rifle to his shoulder. The three men cast anxious glances at each other but the menace of the two lawmen was too much. They knew they did not stand a chance. Reluctantly they turned their mounts towards the water.

Ten minutes later they were on Mexican soil riding away from the Rio Grande in the direction of Diaz's encampment.

SEVEN

Knowing the countryside Jim exchanged places with Clem, and led the small cavalcade at a brisk pace. By noon he was starting up a long incline from the top of which they would look into a secluded valley which held Fernandez Diaz's permanent encampment.

Reaching the top of the incline Jim paused while the others caught up. Only a few Mexicans wandered around the encampment of adobe buildings. The rest were finding some respite from the hot sun. Jim was puzzled for he thought that their approach would already have been signalled. Strange that Diaz hadn't a lookout posted on the ridge. Jim's eyes gazed to the right and he smiled to himself when he saw a stirring among some rocks half-a-mile away. A figure appeared and held his rifle above his head as he faced the valley.

Someone must have failed to stay awake.

As the other four riders reached the ridge Jim sent Midnight down the slope towards the buildings. He saw two figures who had been crossing the square below him turn and run quickly towards one of the buildings. A few moments later he recognised the big frame of Fernandez come outside.

Word travelled fast and soon there was a crowd grouped behind Fernandez, all gazing towards the five riders.

'Ah, you found them, Senor Jim,' greeted Fernandez with a huge smile of satisfaction. He did not wait for any explanation from Jim but turned cold malevolent eyes on the gaolbreakers. 'So, you kill my brother.' He glanced over his shoulder. 'Take them!' he ordered.

Fear and alarm showed on the faces of the three men as six Mexicans ran forward towards them.

'Hold it!' yelled Jim as his Colt appeared in his hand and covered Fernandez. Startled, the six Mexicans stopped in their tracks and cast anxious glances at Fernandez. They did not want to disobey him for they knew what the consequences could be but to do as he said now might have the gringo shooting him. 'My wife, before you take them,' Jim rapped, his eyes boring into Fernandez.

A smile broke across the Mexican's face. 'Oh, Senor Jim, don't you trust me? You'd have got her back. But no matter,' he shrugged his shoulders, 'you can have her now.' He glanced at the Mexican beside him and nodded. The man turned, pushed his way through the crowd and ran towards one of the huts.

'Clem,' Jim shot a quick glance at the lawman, 'keep this bastard covered and pull the trigger if he tries anything.'

As Clem trained his rifle on Fernandez, Jim swung from the saddle. Jim ignored the Mexican as he strode towards the crowd. For one moment it seemed as if hostility would hold them but Jim never faltered in his stride and they parted, making an opening towards the hut.

A moment later Kate appeared followed by the Mexican. She blinked for a moment in the bright sunlight and then seeing her husband striding towards her she started to run with the cry of 'Jim!' ringing across the square.

A few moments later she flung herself into his arms and they held each other tightly. She could not speak for the choking feeling which filled her throat and for the tears of happiness and relief which flowed down her cheeks.

'Everything's all right, Kate,' whispered Jim soothingly. 'Have you been all right?'

She nodded her head still pressed close to his chest. She swallowed hard and with a voice scarcely above a choked whisper said 'Yes. I've been all right.'

'Fernandez treat you well?'

'Yes.' She nodded again, then pushed herself away from his chest until she could look up into his face. 'Oh, Jim, I was so frightened for you. I've been nearly driven out of my mind with worry about what was happening to you.'

He smiled reassuringly at her. 'Well it's all finished now. Let's go home.'

Jim turned and, still with a supporting arm around his wife, went back through the crowd. When they reached the group of riders they found a Mexican holding a horse ready for Kate.

'I told you Mrs Jim would come to no harm,' smiled Fernandez.

Jim ignored the remark as he helped Kate into the saddle. Once she was settled he climbed on to Midnight, drew his Colt and faced Fernandez. 'Clem, take Kate out of here,' he called without taking his eyes off the Mexican. He knew in situations like this he could not afford to give Fernandez any chance to manoeuvre.

The Mexican's eyes smouldered with annoyance. He did not like being at the wrong end of a gun. 'Senor Jim, put that gun away. You've got your wife, now let me take these men.' The words came out too smoothly but did not hide Fernandez's real feelings.

'Hi, Hooper, you ain't leaving us!' Alarm sounded in Joe's voice.

'Can't do anything else, Reed,' answered Jim.

'But you got the drop on him. We could ride out of here!'

'I'm letting my wife get safely out of the way,' said Jim. 'I don't trust this bastard, he could…'

'Senor Jim,' cut in Fernandez, 'I don't like what you say. We're friends.'

'No, Fernandez, we aren't and we never were,' said Jim coldly. 'We tolerated each other and had a working arrangement. I wanted to be left in peace and you wanted horses. So we fix it, but we were never friends. And a word of warning – don't ever try to pull something like this again, don't even think about it because if you do I'll let you die slowly.'

A grin broke across Fernandez's face as he completely ignored Jim's words when he was reminded of the prisoners. 'Like I'm going to do to these three gringos!'

The implication behind his words bit deeply into the minds of the three men. Their cries and pleas with Jim fell on deaf ears.

Knowing that Fernandez had heard his words even though he appeared to ignore them and knowing that the Mexican would take no action against him now that Kate and Clem were well away from the encampment Jim started to turn his horse. He stopped it and eyed the three men who were still pleading with him.

'You scum ain't worth taking a chance with. If I let you ride out of here do you think I could rest easy on the other side of the Rio Grande? Besides, I struck a bargain with Fernandez and I don't break agreements.'

He tapped Midnight and sent him into a gallop away from the crowd. He shut his ears to the pandemonium behind him as with excited shouts the Mexicans dragged the three men from their horses and forced them towards three posts at one side of the square.

Midnight's hooves split the earth as Jim thundered after Kate and Clem who were nearing the top of the incline out of the valley. He saw them pause and look back. Seeing him coming they steadied their horses on the ridge and waited for him.

Jim hauled his horse to a halt alongside them. 'You sure you're all right, Kate?' he asked with the concern of a man who loved his wife dearly.

Kate smiled reassuringly. 'Yes, I am. And relieved to have you here beside me, away from Fernandez.' She shuddered.

'He didn't ill-treat you did he?' pressed Jim.

'No. I was treated all right.'

'Good, because if he had…' Jim left his threat unspoken.

'I wonder what Fernandez would have thought if he'd known about the bank money in my saddlebags,' grinned Clem.

'You've got that money here?' gasped an amazed Kate.

'Yes,' confirmed Jim. 'We caught up with

Crazy Joe and his sidekicks in Lakewood. I wanted Clem to head back for Rosewell but he wouldn't hear of it. I'm mighty glad he came along.'

'So am I,' said Kate. Her deep gratitude showed in her eyes as she looked at Clem. 'If you have that money then we'd better get out of here fast,' she added with great concern. 'Fernandez'll make Crazy Joe tell him where the money is.'

Jim stared at his wife with surprise. 'But Fernandez knows nothing about the money. He doesn't know his brother was mixed up in a bank-raid. He doesn't want Crazy Joe and his sidekicks to find out about the money because he doesn't know there is any; he wants to take revenge for his brother's murder.'

Kate shook her head. 'I overheard two guards talking outside my hut one night. I couldn't make it all out but I gathered that Fernandez and Carlos didn't get on and Fernandez wasn't above spying on his brother. Carlos's meeting with Crazy Joe was seen and after Crazy Joe and the others had ridden off Fernandez tried to make his brother talk. Carlos didn't and died so Fernandez went after Crazy Joe but they'd crossed the Rio Grande and the rest you know.'

Jim let out a low whistle and exchanged a sharp glance with Clem. Each knew what the other must be thinking. Crazy Joe and his sidekicks had been right when they protested their innocence.

'Hell, we've handed them over for something they didn't do. Fernandez wanted them because he suspected the liaison between them and his brother and he wanted to know from someone what it was all about.'

'And they'll talk to save their hides,' said Clem. 'And when Fernandez knows we have the money…'

'I think he knows now!' cried Kate with alarm as a piercing scream split the air along the hillside and men in the encampment were leaping into the saddles.

Jim's eyes pierced the distance to the

encampment and he saw three limp figures hanging from the three posts. He cursed to himself but all further concern for what had happened was driven from his mind as a shot whined close to their heads.

'The lookout!' he yelled. 'Hit that cover!' He grabbed Kate's reins and turned the two horses to a group of rocks. Clem was close behind and as two more shots whined overhead they hit the ground.

'We've got to take that lookout quick,' said Jim, 'or we'll be pinned down here until Fernandez and his mob get here.'

'And that won't be long,' said Clem hearing the thunder of many horses rising from the valley.

'I'll try and take that lookout,' said Jim. 'Make him keep his head down.'

The understanding which the two men had had as sheriff and deputy came back. A few quick words and there was no need for more. Clem was into a position to use his rifle in a flash and his shots crashed across the ridge to the other group of rocks. In the same instance Jim dropped below the ridge on its opposite side to the valley. He ran quickly in a crouched position until he saw that he was below the rocks which hid the lookout. He moved up towards them quickly but quietly, thankful for Clem's continuous shooting.

Gaining the rocks he edged to his right. He saw a cleft which would give him his access to the top of the rock on his left. He climbed it quickly. Clem was still firing, keeping the unseen Mexican pinned down. Seizing a momentary break in the firing Jim came out on the top of the rock and raised his arm in a signal to Clem. Clem under-stood and ceased firing. Jim crouched, alert for any movement among the rocks below him. It came in only a moment for as the firing stopped the lookout moved his posi-tion to return fire. With that movement he stepped from the cover which had hidden him from Jim's sight.

Jim straightened and his presence must have made itself felt for the man spun round, his eyes widening in disbelief. Even in the moment of shock his gun came up automatically but he never had a chance to squeeze the trigger. Jim's bullet took him cleanly in the chest and pitched him to the ground where he lay still.

The thunder of hooves was growing louder and a quick glance told Jim that they had no chance of making a dash for the river.

'Clem,' he yelled. 'You take 'em from that side. I'll stay here.'

Clem acknowledged Jim's call realising that they had some advantage in crossfire at a point where the riders would be forced closer together by the nature of the ground.

Jim positioned himself for the best advantage and weighed up the scene below him. Twenty riders were urging their mounts up the slope from the valley and Fernandez was in the middle of them. Jim lined his rifle on the rider on the right of the three who were some twelve yards in front of the others. He waited patiently until he was certain of his shot. He squeezed the trigger gently. The shot cracked across the hillside. He was aware of the rider pitching from his saddle and of another figure tumbling on the left as he lined up on the third rider and squeezed the trigger.

The main body of riders half-checked their mounts when they saw their companions shot out of their saddles, but then spurred their horses on under the cajoling screams of Fernandez who did not realise that two need not be swamped by twenty. In his craze to get his hands on the money which had been in his encampment without his knowledge his reasoning vanished.

Four more riders hit the dust but suddenly, in spite of Jim's and Clem's rapid firing, two reached the ridge. They turned their horse towards the rocks sheltering Clem and Kate. Clem whirled and loosed off a shot which took one rider in the chest. A searing pain tore at his arm and sent him reeling backwards but even as the man, triumph showing on his face, moved in for the kill Clem fired.

A disbelieving expression crossed the Mexican's face and he pitched to the ground.

The respite from one gun gave a momentary advantage to the other riders, among them Fernandez. He gained the ridge with two others and turned towards the rocks where Jim was reloading. Even as he was ramming the last bullet home he was moving to a gap on his right. With his last step he flung himself forward to hit the ground, roll over and come on to his stomach facing his attackers. He fired rapidly. One of the riders shied away as a bullet took him in the shoulder. Another, slightly behind the other two, hauled on the reins when he saw Fernandez reel in the saddle. Jim's gun kept blazing. Fernandez jerked again. He stared straight at Jim, tried to raise his gun but the effort was too much. Jim rolled quickly out of the way of the flying hooves as the animal went past, spilling the bulky Mexican out of the saddle.

Jim's gun came round on Fernandez but in the same instant he realised he would have no need to use it.

The Mexican who had halted his horse at the first sight of Fernandez reeling suddenly turned and put it into a gallop down the slope at the same time shouting, 'Fernandez dead, Fernandez dead!'

The reaction of the other riders was immediate. They broke off the attack and followed their compatriot down the slope towards the encampment.

Jim pushed himself wearily to his feet. He stood a moment looking down at Fernandez then walked quickly to join Kate and Clem.

Tears of relief ran down Kate's cheeks when she saw him but she immediately turned her attention back to Clem's wound.

'Only a flesh wound,' said Clem when Jim showed his concern.

When she was satisfied that Clem's arm would be all right until it got better attention, they mounted their horses. As they moved from the rocks two wounded Mexicans appeared. The riders checked their horses and Jim's hand closed over the butt of his Colt. Then he saw the two men were not armed and he relaxed.

'Fernandez is dead,' he said. 'Tell your new leader I wish to live in peace with him as I once did with Fernandez, and that I will keep him supplied with horses as I used to do.'

'Si, senor,' the two men returned before they started for the encampment.

Jim watched for a moment, thinking that in some way he had repaid the three men whose bodies still hung from the posts. He turned to Kate and Clem. 'Let's ride for Texas,' he said.

The publishers hope that this book has given you enjoyable reading. Large Print Books are especially designed to be as easy to see and hold as possible. If you wish a complete list of our books please ask at your local library or write directly to:

Dales Large Print Books
Magna House, Long Preston,
Skipton, North Yorkshire.
BD23 4ND